TAKEN—BU

*Laura waited alone in the elegant locked room where she
was held captive. The manservant, Anton, who had
brought her here by force, had left. Her cheek, bruised
in her attempt to escape his speeding coach, still ached.
And in her hand she clutched the knife she had secreted
on her person as her sole means of defense against the
fate clearly planned for her.*

But in her mind was a question sharper than that knife.

*Would she have the will to use that weapon when
whoever had engineered her abduction came through the
door to claim his prize?*

*She feared to find out how weak she might be, just as she
feared to learn the identity of the man who had her in his
power.*

*Then the door swung open. Laura's moment of truth had
arrived. . . .*

YOUR OBEDIENT
SERVANT

ELSIE GAGE was born and raised in Kansas City, where
she still resides. A widow and a retired English
teacher, she now centers her life around her two
daughters and five grandchildren. Her hobbies include
needlepoint and gardening.

Torrid Historical Romances from SIGNET

Your Obedient Servant

by
Elsie Gage

A SIGNET BOOK

NEW AMERICAN LIBRARY

NAL BOOKS ARE AVAILABLE AT QUANTITY DISCOUNTS WHEN USED TO
PROMOTE PRODUCTS OR SERVICES. FOR INFORMATION PLEASE WRITE TO
PREMIUM MARKETING DIVISION, NEW AMERICAN LIBRARY, 1633 BROADWAY,
NEW YORK, NEW YORK 10019.

 SIGNET TRADEMARK REG. U.S. PAT. OFF. AND FOREIGN COUNTRIES
REGISTERED TRADEMARK—MARCA REGISTRADA
HECHO EN CHICAGO, U.S.A.

SIGNET, SIGNET CLASSIC, MENTOR, PLUME, MERIDIAN AND NAL BOOKS
are published by New American Library,
1633 Broadway, New York, New York 10019

First Printing, November, 1985

1 2 3 4 5 6 7 8 9

PRINTED IN THE UNITED STATES OF AMERICA

*To another Caroline
and to Anne-Marie*

1
CHAPTER

The day was beginning to fade. Laura should have been hurrying home to attend Lady Danville, but this part of the home wood was not to be hurried through. She must pause to catch the black shadow of a trout distinct on the bottom of the clear stream, to see the alders, ivy-grown, hanging over the water, and the print of a hare's foot in the moist earth. Here an old beech had broken off; wood sorrel with its white flower had taken root in it. Blue-winged jays flew in and out of the beeches.

Seeing the mud clinging to her stout new shoes and remembering the housekeeper's strictures on neatness, she paused to wipe them ineffectually in the tall grass, her half-awkward movements evidence of her extreme youth and her plain black gown revealing that she was a maidservant. Ahead was the deep, green pool made by a widening of the streambed, and the excited scolding of the jays told the girl that the peace of the wood was being disturbed. She continued slowly, screened by willows, and looked ahead as if through a green tunnel to the long expanse of the pool. She stopped, her breath catching, lost in the arresting and beautiful sight before her.

A moving figure was cleaving the water, his arms

rising and falling in silent precision. The light shone
on the long length of his body, smooth as a seal, and
on his silky dark head and chiseled features as he
approached the nearer end of the pool. Powerful as
engines, his arms rose and fell as he reversed
himself.

Laura fell back as fast as she could. She had the
feeling that something quite dreadful would happen
to her if she were seen. She ran in an oblique path
toward the great house, more breathless because of
what she had seen than from her pell-mell haste.

The mansion was a large one, for three centuries
the seat of the earls of Danville. No one seemed to
have a count of the number of rooms. Built of a
rosy-hued stone that seemed to blend with the
landscape, and with a magnificent prospect, it was
set in a vast reach of fertile acres.

As she stepped into the back entrance, Laura was
welcomed by the tousle-haired house dog, Pax, a
cross between a Bedlington and a deerhound. Followed by the dog up the back stairs to her little
third-floor room, she collapsed onto a wooden chair,
her heart still going like a trip-hammer, half-
fascinated, half-fearful at the scene she had wit-
nessed in the wood. Having spent all her life on a
small farm until a year ago, she was completely
unworldly, and Lady Danville, the mistress of the
house, would see to it that the girl retained that
innocence. Laura still looked like a girl, still enjoyed
only homely pleasures, although her horizon had
widened considerably in the last year. As Mrs.
Meers, the housekeeper, had confidentially opined to
the butler, "The little gudgeon don't know buckram
from burlap, and it's my belief my lady means to
keep her that way."

But Lady Danville's intention was that the child

be given an opportunity to develop a personality that had charmed her on first sight. It had given the older woman an occupation and a challenge. Lady Danville was a self-contained person whose point of view originated in herself, never from custom or from another person. She walked by the light of her own reason and observation. She was accomplished, wise, and gentle, but delicate health had forced her retirement to Glendon from the world of fashion in London that she had graced for years. There, in the absence of her son, the present earl, she had renewed her interest in household and estate management, and a year ago, she had taken under her wing this daughter of a cottager in the nearby village.

"Mrs. Meers says you'm to go to the sewing room and hand-stitch till a tray's brought up, madam's orders, she says." Tess's head peered in at Laura. "And Mrs. Meers won't like them mucky shoes, miss," the upstairs maid went on.

Laura started up from the chair. "Yes, Tess. But am I not to attend her ladyship first?"

Tess looked astonished, then smug. "Only think! I guess you ain't heard the news. The lord's home from his travels. Madam will be busy with him. You ain't ever seen him, I take it?"

"N-no," replied Laura weakly, feeling as if a hand were closing on her throat; perhaps she had seen him that afternoon.

"A proper one. Up in his stirrups, Jed says. Already had the steward call in, and him comin' out of the study lookin' like a poker been run down his back. Mrs. Meers says his lordship ain't one to be trifled with, we all better step lively."

"Yes, well, I am sure she is right," replied the girl in uncertain tones, aware that her life must certainly change with this dreaded arrival of the master,

certain to be one and the same as the man she had
seen in the pool, she thought with a shiver.

Laura Adams had grown up on a small farm near
the village of Dolton. The Adams family had farmed
it for several generations, and the living from it had
not allowed for many luxuries. The Adams were
childless and in their late forties when something of
a miracle happened to them. Coming out into the
farmyard early one summer morning and heading
for the barn to feed the poultry and pigs, James
Adams had been startled to see a white netting tied
to the four posts of the ancient tumbril wagon
standing in the yard. There, in the steep-sided
two-wheeled cart, lay a sleeping baby securely
wrapped in a plain wool blanket.

Sarah Adams, having long ago given up her hope
of mothering a child, had been entranced with the
tiny marvel, with the red-gold curls and the small
waving hands and feet. It was a girl, and in no time
she had entwined herself around the hearts of the
couple, whose greatest fear was that someone would
come to reclaim the child. Inquiries came to nothing.
No stranger had been seen in the nearby village of
Dolton on the previous day. No note or identification
was concealed in the homespun clothing inside the
blanket. Henry Cole, proprietor of the George in the
Borough Inn at the next village of Dorsey, had
indeed served a traveler on the critical day, but he
had shaken his head when questioned.

"Ye're barkin' up the wrong sycamore if ye think
that cove could have a baby hid," he affirmed stoutly. "Druv up in a musty old gig, baited his nag, then
set hisself down with a bottle of brandy. Lurched out
of here drunk as a wheelbarrow."

And so Laura had grown up on the farm, every
year seeing the plants rise from the earth and

flourish. Milking, weeding, the plowing in October, the wheat sown broadcast in the spring, the threshing of corn in the barn—these were all familiar chores to her. She knew little about the proper use of the knife and fork, but she grew strong on the grayish bread and a bit of bacon, eaten off a wooden trencher and washed down with milk or with mead made of honey and yeast. A treat once a month might be a pike stuffed with a pudding in its belly or a boiled neck of mutton. She had a natural and happy childhood. Her education, restricted to a bare learning of her letters at the village school, might be scanty, but from Sarah Adams, a sensible and religious woman, she received good principles, steadiness of character, and a nice tone of mind.

One does not miss what one has never known, and so Laura was unaware of the monotony of the daily round and the daily diet. Toil was taken for granted, with few and simple pleasures. She might catch a glimpse of a silk cravat at the Sign of the Hart in Dolton, but the smock-frock of the farmer or the paper cap of the carpenter were the common uniforms she saw.

When Sarah Adams became ill, Laura's childhood came to an end. During an uncommonly cold and frosty January, Sarah contracted a cold. She remained in good spirits for a while, but in early February she died. James Adams was distraught, and the grieving and bewildered Laura saw him also begin to fail. He appeared to have suffered a stroke, his speech having slowed and his leg dragging to such a degree that it became almost impossible for him to do the farm duties, lighter though they were at this season of the year.

It was at this time that Laura's situation came to the attention of Lady Danville, brought to her notice by the vicar of the church in Dolton, where the earls of Danville had always had the patronage. After several visits, and after her sympathy had been aroused by the plight of the girl and by her loveliness, an arrangement had been made for the care of James Adams in a cottage owned by the Danvilles in Dolton, and Laura had been removed to the mansion house. There she had been assigned humble duties at first, but it had not been long before the mistress of the house took increasing notice of her and formed a resolve to further Laura's education.

It was true that her life was to change now that Lord Danville was at home. In the following days Laura rarely saw her mistress. Her time was spent mostly in the sewing room. Here she studied her texts and drilled herself in the lessons of deportment and proper behavior that had been set out for her. Besides her books, she kept on with her painting and fine sewing, although much time was devoted now to plain sewing for the household. From the plainspoken Mrs. Meers and from Tess, Laura heard the news of the household.

Activity was stepped up tenfold. The number of horses and vehicles in the stables had doubled. The butler, Yeats, answered the door twenty times a day to visitors and messages. Lord Danville thought nothing of inviting his cronies at a hunt or gaming party to Glendon on an instant's notice, and Mrs. Vera, the cook, had added four helpers to her kitchen staff.

Lady Danville came to the sewing room one morning, a look of radiance on her pale features. "For you cannot know, Laura, how it cheers me to see my son. Strict in some of his notions he may be, but he is all consideration and kindness to me. However, I do not wish to bring to his attention that I have made a pet of you; he would be sure to forbid it in the belief that I am overexerting myself. Besides, to be quite frank with you, he has strong opinions on the subject of educating people beyond their stations in life—a deal of foolishness, I call it, but there is no changing him."

"I must thank you for the time you have already spent with me. I can only try to deserve it," Laura said.

"You have pleased me with your progress. Your speech and accent have improved wonderfully in one short year. And now, my dear, the plan of your studies seems to be as good as possible. Trace out for yourself the different branches of literature, taking books from the library. Keep on with mathematics, they accustom the mind to get at the truth, and logic teaches it to reason. The classics never should be forgotten, they give taste and elegance to the mind."

"I shall remember your precepts, my lady," answered the girl gratefully. "May I ask one favor? I would like to continue a weekly visit to my father."

"You must, naturally, and he will receive the sum I set aside for him every month. I only wish that I might give him the cottage outright, but that authority I do not have. Meanwhile, I am persuaded you can understand my decision that you do not come to the particular notice of my son. Mrs. Meers will cooperate in this."

"I shall stay out of his way, ma'am," Laura assured her, thinking with a shudder of that forbidding countenance she had glimpsed.

"Well, I shall miss discussing a pot of tea with you," declared the lady, turning to go. "Most vexatious! But I shall come to visit you frequently, to see how you come along."

2
CHAPTER

Lady Eleanor Danville sat at her tambour frame in the rectangular drawing room. Several pieces of rosewood and mahogany from John Gee in Wardour Street had recently been added, and the room, with its typical Adam fireplace, its furniture in the tradition of Sheraton and Vile, was of the first style of elegance. Three Claudes, a Rembrandt, and a Raeburn looked down from the newly recased walls, and rose velvet hangings set off the long windows.

Her tall son, in ruby-coated hunting attire and plainly having just returned from that absorbing pastime, strolled into the room.

Lady Danville carefully set the needle in her crewelwork and turned to him, the fond look she always wore for him lighting up her fine dark eyes. "Early, Evelyn? No kill today, I take it."

"Damned fox ran through a herd of cattle. Lost the scent, even though we were following Charlesworth's hounds. Best pack in the county." Thomas Fitzhugh David Evelyn, Earl of Danville, disposed his long frame in a gilt armchair.

"Why are they so?" inquired his mother.

"No raw dogs there, yelping at nothing," he said, the indulgent smile he gave her easing for a moment the formidable cut of his mouth and chin. "The pack

14

runs evenly together—no loitering, all due to Charlesworth's training."

"Yes, to be sure, Julian Charlesworth is as perfect in that as in aught else," his mother observed in a rallying tone. "Impeccable lineage, as handsome as Satan, and what you call a complete hand."

"Come, Mama, have you taken Julian in affront?"

"Certainly not. I merely deplore the fact that you and he seem to have taken a joint resolve to keep bachelor hall together."

The Duke of Charlesworth owned an elaborate hunting seat in Dorsey, a nearby village, and he and Lord Danville had been friends since before they were breeched. Together they had taken the Continental Tour and had lingered long in Florence—not solely for the purpose of admiring the architecture, it had been rumored, but also for dallying with the affections of two stunners they had had the good or bad fortune to fetch up with. After nine months of travel to various capitals in Europe, tired of moving about and sated with numerous adventures, they were now ready to rusticate, preferring to forgo the delights of London for a Season. Lord Danville, concerned about his mother's health, had resolved, too, to spend more time with her.

"We like being married to a single life, Mama," remarked Danville, lazily swinging his booted foot.

How handsome he is, thought his mother, noting the restless sable eyes under the winged brows and the long-fingered hand resting on the arm of the chair. It was early acquisition to the title that contributed to his high-handed ways, she reflected, experiencing as always a stab of pain. The late earl, so like his son, had died ten years before in a hunting accident.

"When we were last in residence in London, I had thought you rather taken with the Pendleton girl. She was presented at the queen's drawing rooms, I believe, and I collect that you danced with her at many of the *ton* parties."

"Very true," he conceded, observing that, in the light, her auburn hair was now liberally streaked with gray. He had not noticed it before, nor the lines around the beautiful disciplined mouth. "An unexceptionable miss. She was too full of rectitude and platitude for my taste."

"She was a bit of a bluestocking, I will allow. Then there was Miss Meadows, she had a dazzling smile. Her teeth were as white as alabaster, and her profile was lovely."

"And if it were not for changes in the weather, she would not have been able to start a conversation," he stated with a bored air, his eyes suggesting that he had seen everything there was to see and thought little of most of it. "Next you will be telling me that I should be presented to Lady Vaughan's niece, I'll wager."

"The very thing! Why did I not think of it?" His mother turned a laughing countenance to him. "I have never met her. Excellently connected, too."

"You can't fob me off there. Knocker-faced, I was told by Selwyn. He was presented to her at Almack's. Says the only place you'll see a face like hers is in a bag of oats."

"What a vile thing to say, to be sure. But I do not mean to pinch at you. Plenty of time yet for you to throw the handkerchief. However, I am glad that Caroline Venner helps the time to pass for you here at Glendon."

"A good sort. Doesn't bore one into a coma," Danville agreed.

Caroline Venner was the daughter of Sir Richard Venner, a near neighbor, and the family had been regularly received at Glendon. Sir Richard was a little solemn and ponderous, to be sure, but his wife made up for that with her fund of animation and social chatter. Her daughter, too, displayed a deal of cordiality and liveliness in company, besides having her share of beauty, enhanced by an aura of careful grooming. Caroline had that subtle and indescribable quality of style, whether encased in a morning dress of muslin or gowned in taffeta for a ball. Lady Danville had long thought that her son had a *tendre* for the girl. Lady Eleanor was of such an amiable and sympathetic disposition herself that in general she found little fault in others, and she had seen nothing in the character of Caroline to go against the grain.

Lady Danville did look with a doubtful eye on Caroline's indulged older brother, Nicholas. Nick Venner was seldom at home: Several years earlier he had taken up residence in Venice, detained there, it was generally known, by Lady Henrietta Pauling, who was living at the Palazzo Rivaldi, having been estranged from her husband. Mr. Brandon Russell had written of the Lady Henrietta that "her dress, or lack of it, and her impudence must amaze anyone. She is a writer of manuscripts—eclogues and articles—and is a craftsman of no mean talent." Her superior talents had not held her admirer faithful, certainly, for he had returned to London to become a member of a tightly knit group of insolent bloods. Care-for-nobodies, forever on the search for new stimulation, Danville's mother had described them, but still her son continued to number him among his intimates.

"Well, at any rate, I know how you detest damsels

who blush and bridle, and Caroline does not do that. I do enjoy the stepped-up tempo since you are at home," remarked Lady Eleanor.

"As long as you yourself do not overdo, *ma mère*," directed her son, rising to lean his wide shoulders against the marble mantel. "Yeats and Mrs. Meers have strict orders to save you any extra burden, and the staff can always be increased."

"Nonsense! I rather enjoy getting up new menus with Mrs. Meers, and both she and Yeats have been with us for so long that the running of the place is second nature to them. That is why I do not quite understand your coming down hard on them." This was said with a reproachful look at him, which went ignored.

"I shan't pluck a crow with you on that, Mama, but leniency is a common failing with the fair sex, and you have your share of it. The servants have become somewhat careless. A raking over the coals will bring them up to the mark. Admit it, it has already done so." He looked at her, a brow raised in inquiry.

"You may be right, but I see no need to rap Mr. Farrell over the knuckles. He is a loyal steward."

"He works like a cart horse and has been thinking like one. Partly my fault, of course. I shall prod him out of his ditch, I hope. Ideally, landholders should be resident, attached to the soil and known to every farmer and laborer."

"In what does he err?"

"I come home, Mama, and I see the slow decay of good land under bad husbandry. Barley in the south plot this year means barley in the same plot for next year. Very little rotation of planting, no proper fertilizing. Farrell's reading a few pamphlets on agronomy every evening now, I'll wager."

"Nothing gets by you," said his mother dryly. "It was the same with your father. But I tell you to your head, my dear, you are becoming too top-lofty."

"It's why I suffer from migraine, ma'am," he said, his mouth thinning in self-derision. "The halo gets devilish tight."

And so, despite his mother's remonstrances and reproving looks, the earl had his way. The square face of Yeats became even more somber than formerly, and the footmen now stood to very precise attention. An uncomfortable-looking Mrs. Meers, after more than one summons to the study, lined up the housemaids for weekly inspection and review, and Mrs. Vera became more enthusiastic and inventive in the kitchen. Mr. Farrell tried his hand at cajoling the stubborn tenant farmers out of their feudal ways and was able to report some progress to his exacting employer.

"I'm not complaining, Mr. Yeats," Laura heard Mrs. Meers declare, "for we've known the master since he rode his first pony, but me rheumatism is coming on me something cruel lately."

"That will do, Mrs. Meers," the butler reproved, pokering up. "His lordship's to be obeyed, and we'll have no argle-bargle about it."

It was no wonder, then, that Laura found herself more or less ignored. Lady Eleanor came occasionally to tutor her in mathematics or to encourage the reading program. Once a week, on Friday, Laura made her way to her father's cottage, keeping off the main road and hopping ditches or ducking under fences. She greeted an occasional laborer or villager, but managed to keep herself unnoticed. In fact, the routine of her days began to drag, and curiosity urged her to take little forays from her third-floor captivity. One dreary afternoon, she determined to

slip down to the second floor and take a peek over
the gallery into the flagged hall below.

Tripping down the back stairs, she came to the
gallery that extended on each side of the huge
entrance hall and over whose massive railings six
superb tapestries of antiquity and great value had
been hung. Here in the gloom she might kneel down
and conceal herself behind the hangings should
anyone below raise his eyes to the unused balcony.
There was little likelihood of this, and Laura was
able to peer down into the great hall, seeing the
mahogany staircase, beautifully turned in twists
and spirals, and the bronze-studded entrance doors,
two footmen in attendance nearby. Immediately
below her was a huge table veneered with burr
maple and inlaid with brass. Several formal chairs
japanned in black and gold stood against the walls.

Some sound seemed to have alerted the rigid
footmen below, and they moved as one to open the
massive outside doors. Laura caught a glimpse of
the portico outside and sank in back of a tapestry
around which she could see with perfect safety. A
slight figure attired in a filmy lavender gown entered, closing a parasol of the same hue, so that
Laura could see a head of luxuriant dark hair,
looking as if each raven curl had just been carefully
put in place. The gown was exquisite, and a fold of it
was held with dainty precision in one small hand.
She turned smoothly, waiting for an attendant to
follow.

"You may take the parasol, Banks. Hold the
bonnet ready in case a breeze should come up when I
am ready to leave." The young lady spoke in an
expressionless monotone to a figure who seemed to
be a gray-haired abigail following her mistress. The

servant curtsied, received the parasol, and took herself stiffly toward one of the side chairs. Laura's attention then went to the figure emerging from the drawing room, and her heart upped its beat. It was Lord Danville.

Tall and lean, he moved with lithe grace toward the young lady, his bow perfection. "My mother awaits, Caroline. How very presentable you look, as always." There must have been amusement in his face because Laura could hear indolent amusement in his voice. She could see his smooth dark head, the broad shoulders in a fitted coat of drab-cloth, the tight-fitting breeches, and the burnished boots.

"One moment, Evelyn." The dainty hand came out to touch his coat fleetingly, and the soft voice went on, "About last evening, I was sorry that we—"

"The servants, ma'am," he interrupted blandly, turning to eye the abigail and the two footmen. "Where is Yeats?" The tone had sharpened as he spoke to the footmen.

"My lady said as he was to direct the glazers that is working in the game room, my lord," replied one of these menials.

His attention again on the visitor, he murmured to her in a low tone and saw the lady tap his arm in a familiar manner. "For shame, Evelyn, it is not to be thought of."

A delicate hand then gestured toward the maid-servant, who immediately left her place to curtsy before her mistress. A low-voiced instruction followed, and before Laura could collect herself, the maid was mounting the stairs and making for the balcony. The earl, meanwhile, had dismissed the two footmen with a snap of his fingers. What went on

below after that escaped Laura completely. She
could only crouch down beside the tapestry. The
thin-as-a-rail abigail, Banks, having reached the
balcony, took possession of a tall chair, holding the
bonnet and parasol gingerly and looking straight
before her, evidently having no curiosity about her
surroundings.

This curious hiatus went on for some time, sounds
of muffled conversation coming up from below and
Laura holding herself unmoving. At length the
sounds below ceased. The servant appeared to be
nodding, and the girl rose, fairly certain that she
could slip past her. Tess or Mrs. Meers would
be remarking her absence. But Laura had barely
crept past the dozing maidservant when the
woman awoke with a start, her hand going to her
mouth.

"Is it time? Has Miss Caroline asked for me?"

"No, nobody has asked for you," assured Laura,
relieved that the abigail seemed to see nothing odd
in her own presence there. "You have fallen asleep
for a short while."

"Well, I don't sleep all that much," the woman
apologized, inspecting the bonnet to be sure that it
was not crushed. "A good thing you got me broad
awake now, miss." The maid straightened her thin
back, the cords in her neck standing out.

"I am going up for my tea. Perhaps you would like
me to bring you a cup, along with a biscuit or two?
I'll be back in a trice."

And over a cup of tea the servant became confid-
ing. From what Laura could ascertain, the poor soul
seemed to be run off her feet, required to be in
continual attendance on her young mistress. In the
morning hours she attended to Miss Caroline's

wardrobe. When the lady went anywhere, day or night, her maid was required to attend her, carrying with her anything needed to repair a fault in Miss Venner's perfect grooming.

"To be sure," Banks said to Laura with a kind of pride on her wan face, "it's said not another young lady can come up to her style."

"That may be," replied Laura, "but I doubt it's worth it. You look quite done up."

And as she went off to her third-floor retreat, she recalled that Miss Venner was praised by many of the servants and was regarded as the possible future mistress of Glendon. Laura had heard enough now to be suspicious of Miss Caroline's good nature. Her beloved Lady Danville might come to regret it if Miss Venner should become mistress there.

Having seen so much on her first venture to the gallery, Laura could not resist returning to watch the comings and goings in the house. She learned the names of many who called or left cards: the haughty Duke of Charlesworth; Mr. Brandon Russell, known for his wit and elegance; the Venner family; the lively Duchess of Crawley, who called on Lady Danville; and certain red-faced squires and their ladies who stood uneasily in the hall, waiting to be asked into the drawing room. The dominating force in these scenes was the figure of Lord Danville, moving sometimes with ceremonious grace, sometimes with swift impatience or with ill-disguised boredom.

There is something sinister yet splendid about him, thought Laura. She began to know the shades of his voice and the changes in its tone. Then one day she knew that he was in the hall before she turned

her head to see who had come in. The realization
was frightening to her. She knew that had the hall
been crowded with people or as dark as night, she
would have felt through a sixth sense the instant
when he entered.

3
CHAPTER

Laura rose from her knees, shaking down the black skirt she had hiked up. Every Friday she cleaned in the cottage that Lady Danville had given for her father's use. Sitting in his wooden rocker, her father would ramble on, often about the past, while Laura went about her tasks. A motherly woman, Mrs. Moffitt, glad to earn a few extra shillings to help feed her hungry brood at home, came every day to bring him a portion of hearty soup or a shepherd's pie.

"I am as willing to labor as always, but, alas, I can no longer do it, and you must be the staff of my old age, girl." James Adams spoke slowly and shook his grizzled head.

"That I will, Father, but through the goodness of Lady Danville, we shall go on splendidly. She declares her firm intention that you shall be cared for." Laura pressed his hand and sat down to mend his homespun coat.

"She has taken good care of you. Widow Barron talks of what a genteel girl you are become."

"I try to learn what my lady assigns, but I shan't be setting myself up in the world."

"Nor should you, but ever remember the lessons you learned at your mother's knee." He looked at her with concern.

"I shall, Father, for they are the same principles that Lady Danville holds before me."

"All is well as long as my lady lives," the old man remarked glumly. "But what happens should she catch an illness, as your good mother did? For she is never in blooming health."

Laura heard these words with dismay. They echoed certain fears that she herself had. But lately Lady Danville's energies had revived, and surely the country life she now lived was restoring her strength.

"Do not worry, Father," she said bracingly to the old man. "In any case, you and I will never lack a peat fire to sit over together."

But as she left him and crossed the pasture nearby on her way home, worry over her mistress took over her thoughts. Laura had no self-seeking in these reflections; she only prayed that Lady Danville's goodness continue to guide the many around her who depended on her.

Laura had always been tempted by the vicar's garden, and now she stopped to gaze with remembered longing at the apricots against the wall and the strawberries under their netting. With lagging feet she passed through a copse of tall oak trees. These trees had always fascinated her; she thought there were no such oaks anywhere else, none so tall and erect and with such enormous heads.

The previous Friday she had had a small adventure here. In a thicket in the wood where young saplings grew, she had seen a well-grown boy engaged in some furtive activity. From behind a tree Laura had watched him complete whatever he was doing and then run stealthily away. When she came to the spot, she saw that the boy had laid a fairly ingenious trap of fine mesh, hoping to catch a rabbit, perhaps. Having a great deal of sympathy for the small creatures of the woodland, the girl had taken up the snare and had disposed of it later in the dustbin at Glendon. But today she saw no evidence of the boy's poaching.

When Laura came out of the timber into the open, she had a glimpse of a man on horseback at some distance, and then her eyes became fixed on a huge brindled mastiff that bore down on her. Ordinarily unafraid of dogs, she paused. This creature had a purpose and fierceness about him that caused her to stop in her tracks. The dog came close, its lips drawn back from formidable teeth. A whistle from the distance caused it to draw back a little, but when Laura dared to move, its ferocious snarl made her change her mind.

Out of terrified eyes, she saw its master come near on foot, his horse tethered to a tree. It was Squire Wedlow—Laura had seen him in the hall at Glendon, waiting for Yeats to present his name in the drawing room. His wife had been with him, uneasily patting her fat, brown curls. He had nudged her, adjuring her to stand still and to try not to look like a bottle-head.

"So here's a pretty poacher," he now said gruffly. "Back, Brin. But watch her, boy." The dog sat on its haunches, still growling deep in its throat.

"I—I have been to see my father. I am on my way home to Glendon," Laura finally got out. "I—I often come this way."

"So my bailiff tells me—on Fridays," he stated, his close-set eyes examining her insolently. "And last Friday he saw you come out of my copse carrying a trap. I've had a deal of poaching there, and now there'll be a stop to it. Caught red-handed you are. The earl will hear of this."

"Oh, no!" protested Laura. "I saw a boy laying a snare and I took it after he ran away. I put it in the dustbin at Glendon."

"Quick thinking, but it won't fadge." The squire looked rather preoccupied, his eyes on her exquisite face as he stepped close to her. Laura retreated, and the dog stood up with a threatening growl. "Stay put, little fool, or Brin will go for that pretty throat."

Laura shuddered and looked bravely up at him. "I have done nothing wrong, believe me."

"I've a good notion to have you up for trial," he said, but seeming all the while to be thinking of something else.

The prospect of such a dreadful turn of events so overwhelmed the girl that her limbs felt weak. She only wished that the ground would open and swallow her. What was the use of protesting her innocence? The squire seemed oddly determined to believe her guilty.

"I can do nothing but ask your mercy," she whispered at last, while the squire looked at her in long contemplation.

"Ye may have that, providin' ye learn to eat humble pie," he finally said.

"What do you mean?"

"You'd like this all hushed up, wouldn't ye?" he asked. "Nothing said at Glendon to cause ye to lose your place, and no charge brought before the justice of the peace."

"Yes," she answered dully.

"Then ye'll pay me for silence with a few hugs today—and getting off cheap it is—but I've overdue business in Dolton today. I can't tarry. Next Friday ye'll meet me in the wood here and stay awhile. Then we'll see for sure whether I take ye before Sir John Winton's court."

Laura closed her eyes to blot out the sight of his mouth and his gloating eyes. But she must endure his touch in order to get away.

"Remember the charge can be brought next week same as this, so I'm certain ye'll be real prompt next Friday."

"Yes." I hope to die before I come next Friday, he's a dolt not to know it, thought Laura as she braced herself for his revolting embrace, which could not be avoided.

"By Jupiter, you're a tempting piece. I've a mind to let my business go. We'll see," he mumbled as he drew her seemingly unresisting form toward him, the dog watching alertly.

Laura buried her face against his waistcoat as he enveloped her in a kind of bear hug, but her hands could not resist pushing hard against him.

"No flummoxing me, now, or it's the worse for you," he ordered, breathing heavily, his hand beginning to search out the outline of her figure in the heavy black gown. His other hand was seeking to raise her face to his.

Laura's teeth bit down on her lower lip, but she was unaware of the taste of blood in her mouth. There was a roaring sound in her ears, and through that noise she heard the cool tones of another voice—a dreaded voice that she recognized. Squire Wedlow had miraculously let go of her.

"I intrude at a wrong moment, Squire. You'll excuse it, but the lass is wearing Glendon livery."

Laura opened her eyes an instant to glimpse the earl astride a huge bay, looking down lazily at both of them. The empurpled squire had turned away; he seemed deprived of speech, and Laura reclosed her eyes against this newest and most unbearable calamity.

"You are in service at Glendon?" Laura could barely nod. "Speak, please."

"Yes, my lord," the whispered answer came.

"I dislike interrupting, Squire, but the wench has no business being here." He had turned toward the squire, who, his color faded, drew himself up and made an attempt to appear composed.

"The girl comes trespassing here right frequent-like, my lord," he rasped out.

"And for no good purpose, I see," commented Danville with a sardonic glance in Laura's direction, who stood with folded hands, her eyes on a shining black boot in the stirrup.

"I've not spoken to her before today," put in the squire defensively, "but she's a forward miss. My bailiff reported her thieving ways to me."

"Thieving, you say? You'll have to tell me of it. As for you, girl," he instructed Laura, "return to Glendon at once."

But Laura knew that the squire would blacken her in every way that he could in order to clear his own image with the earl. Her anger against the squire gave her the courage to face his lordship for a moment. She turned toward Danville, the burnished hair thick on her neck. "It's a Banbury tale that the squire will tell you, my lord. Truth is stranger than fiction, and in his case I am sure it's scarcer."

She saw the remarkable dark eyes narrow on her, whether in surprise or in displeasure she could not tell. "Return without delay," he repeated coldly, and Laura turned on her heel, a sob catching in her throat.

She ran—across fields, up hills, through the home wood—as fast as she could. She was in the briars now for sure. And how was she to tell her ladyship what had happened? She had endangered her father's position, too. Laura knew that her lady would believe her. Surely she would use her influence to see that the squire's charge of poaching was dropped. But the earl thought the worst of her; he would not keep her in service even though Lady Danville should defend her, thought the miserable girl as she crept up a back stairs.

Mrs. Meers found her face down on her bed, with her eyes red from weeping as she turned them on the concerned woman. "What's amiss with you, my pretty? The mistress won't be liking it when I tell her you're all to pieces like this."

"I'm in a scrape, Mrs. Meers. Do you suppose my lady would see me? Please, Mrs. Meers, whisper a message to her."

"Well, then, I'll see if I can put a flea in her ear, if you'll put a good face on to show her ladyship, miss."

When she came into the room shortly after tea-time, Lady Danville saw that the girl had steadied herself, but that she still was at a low ebb. "And what had put you into such a pelter, child? Is it your father?"

"Oh, no, ma'am. It happened after I visited my father. I have ruined all, besides having gotten your ladyship in trouble, too." And she haltingly told of the horrors of the afternoon with the squire and of Lord Danville's coming upon the two of them. "I was discovered in the worst possible situation. I have to say it, ma'am, the squire is a wicked man."

Lady Danville had put on a grave face, but she smiled faintly now. "I make no defense of the squire, Laura; he is obviously underbred. I do regret that the earl should see you in such an unpleasant light. It is very likely that he has jumped to false conclusions regarding you."

"I fear so, my lady," agreed the girl, paling.

"We must put as good a face on it as we can. My son is probably well aware of the squire's shortcomings, you know, and he saw that you are but a green girl, after all. I am glad to have previous notice of what to expect, however. I shall be ready for his inquiry into the matter, which is sure to come. Remember always that I believe in you. Meanwhile, oblige me by keeping up your spirits and showing me that steadiness of mind that I have admired in you."

Laura could only return a speaking glance of gratitude and nod dumbly as Lady Danville patted her cheek encouragingly.

Not much time was to elapse before Lady Danville was put to the question. Before the evening meal, which was late, as his lordship kept town hours at Glendon, his mother found him in the study at his wide writing desk. Impeccable in evening attire, an amethyst set in the gleaming folds of his cravat, he stood as she entered.

"A little Madeira, Mama?" He waited for her to take a chair and filled her goblet. He himself had at his elbow a bottle of claret into which he continued to make inroads. "I sometimes wonder if the later hour of supping agrees with you."

"I do not mind, I assure you," she declared. "I now have such a lavish tea that I eat more than formerly."

"All to the good, then. I was abroad late today and had to miss tea. Perhaps you can tell me, ma'am. I came across one of our serving wenches today— quite young, luxuriant lightish hair, blue eyes—who is she?" Although he looked rather bored, the lady thought, Now we're for it.

"It was Laura. She is quite young and light in coloring."

"How is it that I have not seen her about? Is she not young to be in service?"

"She will soon be sixteen, I believe. She keeps to herself in the sewing room, where she is quite busy."

"The girl isn't all that she appears. I saw her a mile away from here and in an awkward position, to say the least."

Lady Danville lifted her delicate brows. "I know of it. She goes on Friday to visit her aging father in Dolton. The trouble she ran into was not of her making. She is a good girl; that I know."

"Your leniency is showing again, Mama," he smiled. "No doubt the girl has deceived you, but I am not so easily gulled. We cannot oversee the morals of the servants, certainly, but a girl that young should be under her father's supervision."

"Squire Wedlow is something of a bounder, you know."

"Probably. He is of the opinion that the girl has been poaching on his land. I believe that he became interested in other matters, however. The girl is a pretty-enough creature, and the squire was tempted. She seemed willing enough."

"You are all wrong. You must let me set you straight. I have a special fondness for Laura, which I have concealed from you."

"Indeed?" His black brows lifted in surprise. "And what is the girl doing on the squire's land? There is a public road to Dolton."

"She was coming from her father's house by a roundabout way." She knew now that she would have to acquaint him with all the circumstances surrounding Laura. And she proceeded to tell him of the depth of her own attachment to the girl and of how she had brought Laura to Glendon and resettled James Adams at Dolton the year before. She then went on to relate the facts of the afternoon as Laura had told them to her.

The earl looked at his mother with incredulity and asked, "Why have you not spoken openly to me?"

Lady Danville could not keep from looking uncomfortable at this, and she answered, "I was certain that you would forbid my taking an interest in her, thinking that I would tire myself in furthering her education. Your views and mine differ, you know, on the value of education for ordinary folk."

"That is true," he admitted, "and the fact that you are already fond of the girl must certainly influence me in any decision regarding her, but understand me, Mama, she is not to be permitted to pull the wool over your eyes. So far, I cannot think well of her. But enough of this set-to. We'll have her down." His ringed hand went to the bell on his desk and Yeats was told to summon Laura.

"And what work does the little angel do in the sewing room, Mama?"

The inquisition begins again, Lady Danville thought wryly. "She does the plain sewing and, besides, has become a fine seamstress. She also studies the lessons I set before her."

"Which include writing and reading, I take it. I noticed the minx spoke in a manner above her station."

"You would be amazed at what a rapid rate she has assimilated every task that is set before her. But before she comes, I must ask that you influence the squire to forget his charges against her." This was said with a speaking look at his hard countenance, and the line of his mouth softened as he returned her entreating glance.

"As you wish, of course."

A knock came at the double doors, and Yeats'

severe countenance appeared. "Laura Adams, your lordship." Into the room slipped the slight black-clad figure of the girl, to curtsy beside the massive doors and to stand with folded hands.

"One and the same girl," Danville said in a sarcastic aside to his mother. "Step forward, Laura."

Laura walked to a spot near Lady Danville, unconsciously taking shelter from the petrifying figure behind the desk. Her eyes lifted as far as the desktop, where his brown hand lay motionless on the polished surface.

"She looks like a little girl—almost, but not quite," he commented dryly, his eyes assessing the lines of her figure. "How often have you encountered Squire Wedlow, Laura?"

"Not before today, my lord," she said through dry lips.

"Your father has been a good and proper parent?" he questioned.

"Yes, sir."

"It might be better for you, then, that you be returned to a father's protection until such time as you are old enough to go into service and can comport yourself with more rationality." He had pushed his carved chair away from the desk and was lounging back.

Laura's cheeks became red as fire at the latter part of this statement. "It was not my behavior today that was questionable, my lord. It was the squire's," she burst out.

A pause ensued, and she looked up to find him looking at her in cool calculation. "We shall give you the benefit of the doubt, at any rate. Squire Wedlow will be asked to overlook the whole incident of the afternoon."

Relief was plain on the girl's face. "Laura will be

allowed to stay on here?" interposed Lady Danville. "I do depend on her, Evelyn."

"Very well. Temporarily, at any rate," he agreed, transferring his dark raking gaze to the girl's flushed face for an instant, "as long as she takes no liberties with those whom she is obliged to hold in respect. She shows signs of perverseness that will have to be subdued. Also, she is to be no burden to you. Let her assume serving duties in the house under Mrs. Meers. However, since you find her person pleasing, ma'am, she may wait on you at certain times to save your strength."

"We must heed his lordship," enjoined Lady Danville to Laura with a kind smile. "I trust you will be agreeable to his commands, for we must all in this house submit to them with good will."

"I shall be happy in any form of service that is required of me, my lady, and I will do as my lord requires."

"Your new duties will be set out later, Laura, and after you have had a good rest, you will feel better. You may leave us now, and I will come to see you tomorrow."

When the door had closed on her, Danville observed carelessly, "She'll improve after she has shed her milk teeth, no doubt."

"You are still half of the opinion that she is not modest and good. You are wrong, but even so, I do not apprehend why male digressions are excusable, and even the smallest variation from rules governing females is unpardonable."

"Very true, ma'am," he agreed, smiling and draining his goblet.

The first indication of Laura's changed status came the next morning as she sat in the sewing room mending a lace cloth. Mrs. Meers entered, and

Laura thought her greeting held a certain confusion and reserve.

"The master had me in, Laura. Ye'll have to change your ways, lass."

"Yes, I was told last evening that I am to look to you for orders, Mrs. Meers." The girl's tired eyes revealed that she had lain long awake, going over that trying examination before Lord Danville. The demeaning phrases that he had used—"comport yourself with more rationality," "she shows signs of perverseness"—had caused her agonies of shame. He had formed a poor estimate of her. But for Lady Danville's sake and for her own sake she would strive with a willing spirit to do what was required of her. She had come off much better than she had hoped. At least now, she thought wryly, there was little chance of getting above herself in the world.

"First, miss, I have this to say. The plain sewing is to be done, but ye can give up the fine seaming and all the bookwork ye've been doing, that's not for you now. The master says you're to be brought to task." Mrs. Meers' gaze was firm but not unkind. She had a fondness for Laura. However, she had accepted the fact that no order of his lordship's was to be deviated from, and Yeats was forever keeping an admonishing eye on her. "Ye can pack up your books and easel. I'll have a footman up to store the things."

"As you say, Mrs. Meers," agreed Laura, hearing with a pang that all her pleasurable pursuits were to be denied her.

"You'll not have time for that kind of foolery now," the housekeeper went on, as if to comfort the girl. "Ye're to be waiting maid to her ladyship when she requires it. But not today; the master's taken her out in the carriage. I'm not putting you to rough work. Ye're too young and ye'll do better serving in the

parlor, what with the genteel ways you've picked up.
Millie's waitin' for you belowstairs. She'll train you
up. Now, it don't exactly suit me to tell you this,
miss, but if you don't please, Yeats is to hear of it.
Mebbe you don't know it, but Mr. Yeats is a high
stickler and follows the master to the world's end.
Why, he's as much the master's man as that valet of
his lordship's, Beccles."

"I am heeding all you say," replied Laura, wishing
that she might have been assigned to the kitchen
and dreading the possibility of coming under the
earl's critical eye in the parlor. But he would probably take no note, one way or the other.

"I have to tell ye all this for your own good." Mrs.
Meers was looking flushed.

"You are kind, and I will try to please." Laura was
smiling her delicate half-smile, which went right to
the housekeeper's heart.

"Well, now, hasten down and get to it. You'll get
used to it quick as the cat has time to lick her ear.
Her ladyship whispered to me she'll be up this
evening."

But it was in the late afternoon that Lady Danville had a few moments with Laura. She came upon
the girl in the drawing room, where Laura was
preparing to lay a fire—Millie was setting her to
simple tasks to begin with. The earl had just seen
his mother into the house and had proceeded on to
the stable with their other passenger, Miss Caroline
Venner. They had spent a pleasant day at Sir John
Winton's estate, where a large party had gathered
for a luncheon to celebrate Lady Winton's birthday.
Miss Venner had been induced, or, possibly, had
artfully made the arrangement to return in the
Danville carriage.

"I hope you are not fagged to death, child," exclaimed Lady Danville now. "I heard from Mrs. Meers this morning, and I regret that we cannot keep on as formerly."

"I shan't fall into a gloom, my lady, I am so relieved that matters did not fall out a great deal worse for me." Laura smiled up from her kneeling position on the hearth. Lady Danville had seated herself in a velvet chair and had thrown back her ruffled pelisse.

"I don't mind telling you that I would like to change matters, but I am at a standstill once the earl gets a maggot into his head. But enough of that. Matters will come about. Perhaps we can gradually resume your studies when all this stir is over; you may be sure that—" The lady quickly silenced herself as two figures appeared at one of the long French windows.

"Really, Evelyn, I shan't be on speaking terms with you if you forbid me an outing on that mare. My lady, you will have to speak up for me." The lisping sweet tones of Miss Caroline Venner were known to Laura, and she knew without turning that the earl had just stepped into the room. She willed her hands to perform their task so that she could the more quickly leave the room. Just let him not notice me, she implored silently.

"Certainly you may ride her, after some of the ginger is taken out of her," he agreed lazily, "for I don't relish having you buzz about me like a hornet over the matter."

"Oh, how absurd you are. Is he not dreadful, ma'am?"

"Beyond the pale, Caroline, you should know it by now. A glass of wine or a cup of tea, my dear?"

Laura rose from the hearth, remembering to drop a stiff curtsy as she turned. One look showed Miss Caroline seating herself on a small sofa and his lordship standing with arms folded regarding his visitor with a kind of detached indulgence. Laura backed from the room. He had not taken any note of her.

4
CHAPTER

The duties of a parlormaid are demanding, Laura discovered, but as she had tackled much harder work on the farm, she refused to fall into a depression over her changed circumstances. Mrs. Meers so much approved of this cheerful acceptance that she was heard to comment to Tess, "There's nothing nip-cheese about that girl's spirit; anyone else would have been in a regular miff-maff."

The footmen took care of the lighting in the heavy chandeliers, using tall ladders to replace the candles, of which over a thousand of the best beeswax were used every month. The parlormaids cleaned and cared for the smaller candelabra. They also kept in order the rare collections of treasures, and Laura was eventually allowed this privilege by Millie.

The collections included bronzes of Greek and Roman origin as well as statues wrought in stone and marble from Pompeii. The fifth Earl of Danville had collected albums of priceless prints and engravings, including many attributed to Raphael and Titian. These were housed in cases of carved ebony and glass.

In the library, books must be dusted and the leather oiled. The shelves there housed first editions such as *Istoria,* bound for Henry IV of France; *Arms*

of the Knights of the Garter, prepared for Queen
Elizabeth; and *Whitley's Artists and Friends,* a present to the late earl from the Dilettanti Society.
Altogether the library held some fifteen hundred
volumes, and in this room Laura had need of self-
restraint, her hand often lingering on a tantalizing
volume and opening it for a glimpse of a page or two.
She was discovered as she stood on a low stool
looking into an old pamphlet that revealed scandals
relating to Mary Queen of Scots, by Yeats, who had
come silently into the room in his prying way. She
started when she heard his dry blighting tones.

"You may step down, miss. We don't permit
slacking off in this household."

Laura's heart sank. So far she had only encountered Yeats' inspection out of a pair of bleak gray
eyes. But she had known that she would receive
short shrift from him should she trip up in her
duties.

"I—I was tempted to look into this pamphlet, Mr.
Yeats. Millie has set me to dusting the shelves."

"And sleeping at the post you are."

"I would not do that. I shan't pause again."

"Are you telling me that you were not idling?"
Yeats had a watchful look, as if waiting to catch her
in an untruth or an impertinence.

"N-no, sir." A long moment followed.

"If I have to give you what-for again, miss, his
lordship will receive a report of it, and no bones
about it." He then went on to inveigh against
do-nothing servants who funked their duties and
alienated their masters. Seeing that she stood respectfully silent during this dressing-down, he finally took himself off and a shaken Laura returned to
her duties.

Other collections in the vast room included an

extensive collection of the soft-paste porcelain,
Sevres, which Lord Danville had gathered in Paris
and had ordered shipped to Glendon. He admired it
because of its beauty and texture, declaring that it
was the highest finished thing of its kind. Along
with an array of enameled snuffboxes, the porcelain
was kept in inlaid satinwood cabinets lining the
picture gallery, and Laura, when the time came to
wash it, did her assigned part with bated breath. In
the gallery was also a case of curios, and the girl
shivered when she accidentally touched the lock of
Mary Tudor's hair, cut when her coffin had been
opened in 1784.

Millie's wizened face hid a kindly nature, the girl
soon decided. Laura was at last graduated to the
task of bringing in the tea cart and setting up the
heavy tea service, a chore she performed reluctantly
because it brought her near the earl and under his
eye. That eye might pass over her as if she were a
post, but she could never be easy under it. Often she
would be dismissed after wheeling in the service,
but at other times she would be required to pass the
cups or trays of cakes, while Lady Danville poured.
Then it was that the cup might rattle in the saucer
as she gave it into his lordship's long-fingered hand.
Once she thought she saw a dark brow raised
critically at her, but when she looked again, his face
had resumed its impassive look. On these occasions
Lady Danville, as much as was in her power, de-
flected attention away from her.

There was one person who began to speak ill of her
to others in the house. It was the angular Bertha
Harris, who had been dresser and maid to Lady
Danville for thirty years. Laura could not blame
Harris, the be-all of whose existence was the love
and devotion she had for her mistress. She had been

supplanted by another in many of the services she
performed, and she saw herself cut out by a mere
rustic, a "mushroom by-blow," Harris called her.
And since the maid's opinions naturally carried
weight with the lower servants, Laura began to feel
the effect that backbiting can have on a person who
has no defense against it.

It was usually in the early morning or evening
that Lady Danville sent for Laura to come to her
chambers. All the pleasures that she had now were
in those rooms; they expressed the personality of
their owner, with their lovely garlanded ceilings,
light airy draperies, and delicate furniture. Sometimes Laura would rub away a headache or a pain
for the older woman; her fingers had a magic that
eased tension. Or she might polish the graying hair
between the folds of a silk handkerchief. While this
was going on, she received all the benefits that a fine
and mature mind can bestow on a young and un-
formed one. Lady Danville had begun to teach her
French, beginning with simple conversation.

Laura was becoming more mature; her senses
quickened and became more acute. She was discovering that the real meaning of life could be found in
special moments, with whole hours and days of
sameness in between. And now she was being made
aware of the changes in her appearance. Sometimes
she looked with curiosity and a smidgin of vanity
into the mirror at the harebell blueness of her eyes,
at the high cheekbones, and the ripening fullness of
a generous mouth.

She was thrown into confusion, too, by the gazes of
the footmen that followed her slyly. Once she heard
talk behind the baize door of the servants' entrance
that she knew referred to her. "A lusty purty
wench"—"Ay, a meaty sparrow, that one." Joseph

and Oliver, two of the younger grooms, converged on her whenever she went near the stables, attempting to impress her with loud tales of physical prowess, parading ridiculously before her. She had seen so much of that kind of courting among the farmers and villagers: a commonplace surrender to the physical without any hunger of the mind. She did not want to be betrayed into a lifetime of mean stinting of the body, bearing a parcel of children who could have no future better than that of their parents.

Sometimes the earl might stroll unceremoniously into his mother's sitting room. Laura would make a token obeisance and continue with whatever was occupying her, while he teasingly conversed with his mother. His attitude toward Lady Eleanor showed a continuing concern for her welfare. Even a short visit from him made the day bright for the lady.

On one such occasion, he entered while Laura was rubbing away the weariness of the day for Lady Danville, who was reclining on a brocaded chaise. His broad shoulders, impeccably clad in a tan driving coat of superfine, seemed to fill the window embrasure as he went to stand there, looking down frowningly from his great height.

"What's amiss, ma'am?" he asked abruptly. Laura's hands had ceased their movements.

"Very little, really, but I had the beginning of a headache, and Laura's hands are soothing. She is better than a doctor." The lady was smiling up at her. "It is nothing, Evelyn."

"Continue with the treatment, then, since it affords you relief. I will wait," he ordered, folding his arms and leaning against the window frame.

Laura's fingers began their stroking movements but seemed to have lost some of their nimbleness. In her exertions, a coil of her heavy hair had loosened,

and she felt it slide to her shoulder, while color came
and went in her cheeks and her breath shortened.
She did not see his lazy gaze assessing her figure to
the last centimeter, and it seemed an age to her
before he spoke again.

Pax, the house dog, was asleep in a corner of the
room, and roused by a rebuke from Lady Danville,
he came to his lordship's side and was rewarded by a
caress. "The old fellow snores enough to bring the
plaster down," he remarked.

"Yes, he sleeps a great deal now," confirmed his
mother, raising herself to a sitting position. "Thank
you, Laura, I feel refreshed." Seeing with relief that
she was being dismissed, the girl gave an abrupt
little curtsy and made her exit.

"Your maidservant has a kind of awkward grace,
with her curtsies and airs," he observed. "I see that
you have taught her some of the manners of a
gentlewoman. However, you'd do the girl more kindness to put her into the dairy, for she'll be utterly
spoiled for any useful purpose."

"Into the dairy? Absurd! In one short year that
she has had of education, it has done more for her
than a whole life has done for others!" The lady was
beginning to look provoked.

"Enough, ma'am," he said with a laugh, putting
up his hand in the gesture of a fencer acknowledging
a hit. "Let be. The girl's well enough for what she is,
but she will confine herself to serving you and to
working under Mrs. Meers." Seeing that Lady Danville looked chagrined at the latter part of this
statement, he went on to change the subject. It was
clear that he would hear no further protests. "I must
be off to London on business next week."

"How long away?" she asked quickly.

"A good while. Will you not accompany me?"

"No," she answered regretfully. "I am not up to snuff enough for the London whirl."

"You can deny yourself to visitors and invitations, you know."

"Well, I do not wish to bore on about it, Evelyn, but in London I see my friends decaying with age or some malady. The years have deprived me of many whom I knew since childhood and others whom a congenial frame of mind endeared to me. I really prefer a quiet life in the country now."

"Entirely as you wish, Mama," he said understandingly. "I shall come back to check on you now and again."

The earl left for London the following Tuesday, attended by his man, Beccles, and two grooms. Lady Danville observed to Laura that she had not expected him to remain in the country for long; it was natural that, at his age and with his restless disposition, town life would appeal to him. "It is a round of pleasure that he and his intimates have there. Besides a sporting life of fencing, boxing, and horse-racing, he is often at the gaming tables or attending some ball or rout."

Laura listened in wonder to these rare confidences; she had had no conception of what the life of the wealthy and titled in London could be.

There was a lessening of strain and activity in the house now, but the all-seeing eye of Yeats ensured that the servants did not slack off. Laura still continued many of her household duties, but she had increasing freedom to pursue her studies. Some of her books were brought out of storage with a reminder that they would be put away again on the earl's return. Often Lady Eleanor required Laura to sing her a song in her rich low voice or to dance before her. She must also learn to flower and to practice fine drawing. "For my energy won't last forever," the lady declared, "and while I have it, you should proceed to master as many subjects as my poor talents can teach you."

From remarks such as this, Laura suspected that Lady Danville often concealed her aches and pains; she had no desire to inflict them on others. This was made more evident to the worried Laura after a visit from the Duchess of Crawley, who was staying with the dowager Countess of Clayton at the hunting lodge of the Duke of Charlesworth, a nephew of the duchess. The ladies made two excursions to Glendon. On their first call, Laura had been sent to the drawing room to collect the tea tray.

"I cannot imagine that the Prince so far forgets himself," Lady Eleanor was saying, while the petite Duchess of Crawley and her buxom friend, Lady Clayton, were adjusting their shawls for departure.

"You may well believe it," stated the outspoken duchess, "for it has been common knowledge for some time. He is so in love that it is ridiculous. Am I not right, Lucy?" The countess nodded benignly. "She brought her whole family to court, using the horses and carriages from the royal stables. She grows wonderfully haughty, I can tell you."

"Mrs. C. is a commonplace sort of person," said Lady Clayton flatly. "Her husband has been made a marquess and ignores the scandal. But what can you expect from a person with a head like a pineapple?" Neither of her listeners could keep from smiling at this.

"Come, Lucy," interposed the duchess. "Until next week, then, Eleanor. No, do not accompany us to the door. Your pretty maid here can attend us." And while the carriage was being brought around, Laura heard the duchess murmur to her companion.

"I see that her energy flags. I cannot abide even the thought of it."

"What her infirmity is we shan't know; her spirit will not flag, at any rate," responded the countess.

"Exactly. She is a creature of a thousand excellencies." The two ladies were disappearing through the door.

Laura suddenly realized that in the familiarity of seeing her mistress every day, she had failed to see that she had altered for the worse.

It was several weeks before the earl returned, and then his stay at Glendon lasted only for ten days. He was so taken up with following the hunt that Caroline Venner, whose attentions to Lady Danville somehow increased when the earl was at home, declared that she was not going to put up with such Turkish treatment. The young lady then sulked at home for three days until the earl sent a footman off with a missive asking for permission to escort Lady Venner, in her husband's absence, and her daughter to a hunt ball at Squire Barton's in the Grove.

During this time Laura resumed more household tasks and escaped his lordship's eye, she thought. But she was mistaken. He must have seen her from the windows looking into the garden. Pax had aged so much that the old dog had to be forced out twice a day. Laura had always a bad time with him, what with having to coax or carry him along as best she could.

At any rate, Lord Danville had seen enough of her to cause him to speak of her again to his mother. "The wench that runs tame for you, Mama, she begins to mature, and to put it baldly, there is something tantalizing about her."

"I am aware that she grows uncommonly attractive. I must warn her to be careful."

"Careful? Girls of that kind are rarely as chaste as Diana," he observed cynically. "My only wish is to spare you disappointment in her."

"No such thing, Evelyn," she exclaimed sharply, driven to rare anger with him. "I care not whether you believe it or not, but laid deep in her mind are the foundations of piety and modesty."

It was after this that Lady Danville decided to point out to the girl the advantage of prudent behavior; she was afraid for Laura when she saw her growing beauty. One afternoon the lady dismissed Harris, who had been arranging her hair, and only Laura saw the baleful look directed at her by the maid before she quit the room.

"Sit beside me, Laura. I wish to talk awhile. I suppose your mirror tells you how very pretty you have become?" Lady Danville saw the color mount to the young girl's brow.

"I—I have thought very little about it."

"I knew you were too sensible to become puffed up about it, but it is a fact, you know."

"If it is true, I—I can have no praise for it, at any rate."

"It is true enough. I have seen what passes for beauty. Your skin is like rose leaves, and your eyes are like the deep sea." The girl could only look confused at this home speaking. "I do not wish to put you to the blush, but it is necessary to forewarn you. Having seen the world, I know something of men. Yours is the kind of beauty, added to that something in your personality, that would go right to a man's heart—in the manner of Nell Gwyn or a Madame du Barry." Seeing Laura looking at her in blank astonishment, she went on to declare, "I know I am right, and I must warn you to be cautious and somewhat afraid of your own attractions."

"Well, my lady," Laura said in a grave manner, "I hope to stay on the right path, whatever my appearance."

"I do not fear for *your* principles; I fear the dangers you may face and the freedoms that may be taken with you. It is also possible that a time might come when temptation would strain your powers of resistance."

"I would pray that, at such a time, what I had believed in at a previous, more rational time might prevail, ma'am."

"You speak with your usual good sense," smiled Lady Danville approvingly.

5
CHAPTER

I wish I may never live anywhere but here, near Dolton, Laura often thought. From the upper windows at Glendon she could see the distant hills dominated by the rocky outline of Ramstor, whose steep sides she had tried to scale as a child. Another year had gone by: she had seen the hills and fields change from green to yellow; then snow had covered hills and town in a blanket of quiet—noises disappearing, and colors, too. Now it was April, when life quickened in everything, when memory stirred more profoundly.

It had been a good year. Laura had visited her father, run errands, gone for slow walks with Lady Danville, unraveled embroidery silks, listened, and learned. But now Lady Danville had decided to accept an invitation to spend some time with the Venners.

"If I don't stir myself occasionally, I shall become a poor stick. You must come along, Laura, and Harris will attend me. I am anxious to hear the latest from London; Miss Venner and her Mama have just returned from there."

The next day found them on their way, Harris tightening her lips because Lady Danville chose to speak in French to Laura, as she often did. The carriage drew up to the imposing portico of the

Venner residence in midafternoon. It was a large square house built of limestone, its lines softened by a dense growth of ivy. Surrounded by a pretty park dotted with firs, and with a long approach under sheltering beeches, it had a meticulous, well-kept look. Laura was struck with the sudden blaze of red, gold, and green colors against the dark wood of the hall. They were shown into a long drawing room carpeted in crimson, with white velvet hangings at the numerous windows.

"You see how Lady Venner uses color, Laura; the effect is unusual."

Lady Danville had turned to meet Lady Venner, who swept into the room followed by her dainty daughter. "My dear Eleanor, how Caroline and I have looked forward to this visit!"

"Yes, indeed," chimed in Caroline. "You will like to hear that I saw Evelyn only three nights ago; it was at the Devlin ball." The two older women had embraced, and Caroline was sketching a charming curtsy, her afternoon gown of lavender trimmed with heavy Brussels lace a perfect foil for her dark beauty.

"One moment, Caroline darling," Lady Venner interposed. "You have brought two servants, Eleanor?" She was looking in surprise from under her sandy brows at Harris and Laura in the background, noting Laura's unusual attraction.

"Harris is my maid. I also brought Laura, who is my constant companion." Lady Danville motioned the girl forward. The lady often wished that she might purchase a few simple round gowns for Laura —it would have improved her status—but Lord Danville's surprise visits to Glendon forbade any such notion. The instructions he had laid down for the girl must still hold.

"Good. Caroline shall see to them and will also have the ratafia sent in." Lady Venner was escorting Lady Danville to a chair.

"This way, please." Laura and Harris followed Miss Venner's straight back into the hall, where Laura espied the abigail, Banks, seated near the drawing-room doors. Banks started to her feet at once, no look of recognition dawning to indicate that she had talked to Laura previously in the gallery at Glendon.

"You are excused to go on with your work, Banks." Caroline waited impassively while Banks retreated through the servants' door. She then shifted her gaze to the two before her, saying nothing for some time and finally causing Harris to shift nervously from one foot to the other, while Laura became aware that she herself was being minutely inspected.

"You are her ladyship's dresser, Harris. What service does this other servant perform?" Miss Caroline asked, not deigning to question Laura directly.

"She—she is a great favorite of my lady's," mumbled Harris.

"Answer my question, Harris. Do not swallow your words." The lisping voice was gentle.

"Yes, ma'am. My lady—my lady teaches her, and Laura reads to her and such like."

"You may go to the servants' waiting room until you are summoned, Laura. You will share a room with Harris." Laura looked for an instant into a pair of beautiful hazel eyes, eyes that were blank. She had never felt that way before: somehow as if she, Laura, were being erased by another person. She quickly and thankfully made her exit, almost pitying Harris that she must remain under that soulless scrutiny.

A half-hour later Laura and Harris were shown to a good-sized third-floor room by the housekeeper, Mrs. Hedges, who had the same anxious thinness that Laura had noted in Banks. As the door closed on them, Harris turned toward her with a suppressed air of excitement.

"Ye'll find this house is run a little different from Glendon, miss; ye'll march to orders from Miss Caroline here."

"Why, I intend to wait on Lady Danville as usual," said Laura in surprise, "which cannot offend Miss Caroline, surely."

"Miss Caroline is one to give a set-down to them as deserves it. She don't like the look of you."

"And you did not help matters, I'll warrant."

Harris did not reply, turning disdainfully away. Appeal was useless, thought Laura, and now she must have as a chambermate a person who despised her, unless Lady Danville decided that Laura should sleep in her dressing room.

But Lady Danville had developed a cold and would not have Laura exposed to it. Time hung heavy on her hands. Harris was in constant attendance. Miss Caroline took it upon herself to fetch and carry for the guest.

Laura had tried to resume her attendance on her mistress. Two days after their arrival, she was within ten feet of Lady Danville's door when she was arrested by a soft voice behind her.

"Has Lady Danville summoned you, Laura?"

Laura turned to face her gentle questioner, clad in a lacy amethyst morning gown. "No, Miss Venner, but I am anxious to be of help."

Laura could not know that Lady Danville that morning had instructed Harris to summon Laura as far as the door so that she might speak to her. This message had been relayed to Miss Caroline, who had given her orders to Harris.

"Too many people in attendance on an ailing person is not good. Laura will remain ignorant of Lady Danville's request. I shall quiet her ladyship's mind with regard to Laura. You will do well to come to me always while your lady is a guest here."

"Yes, ma'am." Miss Venner had not missed a look of satisfaction on the servant's face.

"I think, perhaps, that Laura puts herself forward. She should be put down," the slow voice continued.

"Yes, ma'am," Harris had agreed devoutly.

Now Miss Venner had caught out the girl, and Laura would squirm for it. Her beauty had aroused instant dislike, and when Miss Caroline's dislike was aroused, she gave free rein to it.

"Servants are not permitted in this part of the house unless summoned," she said quietly, contentedly observing the flush that mounted to Laura's brow. "The matter will have to be called to the attention of my father, Sir Richard."

"I—I was not aware that I transgressed any rules, Miss Venner," protested the appalled Laura.

"You will attend me to his study," decreed the young lady, an inexorable quality in her tone. She had turned away and was walking toward the stairhead, her little forefinger and thumb holding a fold of her gown. Laura followed numbly.

They passed an open door, and Miss Caroline paused. Banks was just emerging from the room and sank into her usual curtsy.

"I believe you had enough to keep you occupied, Banks."

The maid paled. "Mrs. Hedges . . . Miss, she wanted a little help."

The silence was broken only by the tick of a clock. The maidservant seemed to shrink.

"Shall you and Mrs. Hedges need another lesson?"

"No, miss." The servant was biting her lip.

"Come with me, Banks." The slender figure made its way down the broad stairs, followed by Laura and the maid. In the square hall, they could discern Lady Venner, her mousy-colored head bent over a missive in her hand. The lady looked up to call to her daughter with delight.

"Oh, Caroline darling, Nick is coming for a visit."

They had reached the bottom of the stairs, and Laura saw Miss Venner run forward in the first display of real emotion that Laura had seen in her.

"Oh, Mama!" she cried. "When? I cannot wait!"

"You know he would not commit himself to a definite time, child. Mrs. Hedges must get busy; all must be in readiness or he will come down hard on us. But what are you about now?" The lady was looking at Laura and Banks. "Oh, for shame, Banks, have you been remiss again?"

"I am sorry to say she has, Mama. Banks, you may stand here in the hall until I dismiss you to your duties." Miss Caroline watched complacently while the unfortunate Banks took a position near the stairwell. Laura saw that Lady Venner was shaking her head reprovingly at Banks.

"This servant of Lady Danville's puts herself forward, Mama. Papa must speak to her," Miss Caroline went on, her lower lip pouting entrancingly.

"Certainly, my love, you know best. But I wish you will not tire yourself. You have been so occupied with Lady Danville."

"Naturally, Mama, she is such a dear. But do summon Mrs. Hedges to the morning room. We must

think of everything to please Nick!" And throwing a
dazzling smile over her shoulder, she tripped toward
her father's study, motioning Laura to follow.

Without knocking, Miss Venner entered the study,
discovering her father seated at a broad desk in the
center of the room, in close concentration on his
papers. His head jerked up, the dour face taking on
an indulgent look when he saw his slim daughter.
His white hand laid down a pen.

"A morning visit, my love?"

"Well, I am sorry to interrupt you, Papa. I wish
you will reprove this servant of Lady Danville's. You
know how much I have been occupied with Lady
Danville's illness. She also has her maid Harris with
her. Laura here seems to think her presence is
required, even though she has not been summoned."

The habitually stern look on Sir Richard Venner's
face returned as he turned his attention to Laura.
"You have come to the wrong house if you expect to
take freedoms here, wench. My servants know their
place."

"I merely wished to see how my lady went on, sir,"
replied Laura.

"No excuses," he commanded, standing up and
showing a powerful black-garbed figure. "Typical of
her class," he said pompously to his daughter. "She
has health and a certain attraction, which makes
her overstep herself."

"You are right, as always, Papa," smiled Miss
Venner.

"Should it be necessary for Miss Caroline to complain to me again concerning you, you will be sent
back to Glendon at once. Lady Danville cannot be
troubled by such matters."

Afraid that she might be separated from the ailing
Lady Danville, Laura kept silent. But the brake that

she was keeping on her tongue was beginning to be irksome. It was clear that there was something pitiless and unnatural in Caroline Venner's makeup and that the girl held her parents in the palm of her hand.

"Papa! The best of news! Nick is coming, Mama just had word of it." Laura saw the softening in the father's face; it appeared that here was a family where neither the daughter nor the son had ever done a wrong.

"The young rogue! Well, at the rate he has been spending up, it's time he came home. Franking him in Venice was bad enough, and now in London he's been playing ducks and drakes. Well, well, I shall be glad to see him!" He was shaking his head from side to side.

"Well, Papa, you know you never tighten the purse strings with either of us, and it was Lady Pauling who spent most of your money in Venice," she went on with a wicked glance at him.

Sir Richard looked a little out of countenance at this. "Never mind that! Let's hope he doesn't get in one of his cursed gloomy starts while he is here. Meybe we can keep him home awhile. Do you try to cozen him along, lass, he'll often listen to you."

"Rubbish, Papa! He'll only please himself, and you know it!"

"Be that as it may, I hope you will stir up some activity to keep the rascal amused. You'll know how to go about it, my pretty. And no doubt he'll lure some of his cronies from London down here to the country." He was smiling benignly at her.

"Of course, Papa. Mama and I have already summoned Mrs. Hedges." Caroline, all animation gone from her face, turned to the waiting Laura. "You may return to the servants' quarters. No idleness will be allowed, however. Mrs. Hedges will instruct you."

The cold stare of Sir Richard and the unfeeling eyes of Miss Venner followed Laura as she left the room. How glad she would be when Lady Danville returned to Glendon, she thought. She would have to walk softly in this house. She knew that Caroline Venner would do her a harm if she could. Harris, busy with mending in the room they shared, looked hard at her when she entered.

"I reckon Sir Richard and Miss Caroline gave you what-for; she don't like a brazen face."

"You'll do well to curb your tongue, Harris. You might drive me to speak to Lady Danville about you."

The maid cast her eyes down and assumed an injured air. "It's only that I want to do what's best for the mistress."

"I understand you and your motives perfectly." The girl shrugged a slim shoulder. "Now, tell me, how is my lady?"

"She does well enough and will do better when she begins to eat more, the doctor says," replied Harris reluctantly.

In the afternoon Laura was put to work in the kitchen. A wondrous variety of meats, pastries, and sauces had been ordered for the return of the prodigal. Laura learned that the young master had arrived, bringing two of his friends. When she was sent to the dining hall with a tray of crystal glasses, she heard shouts of laughter from the game room as she passed it.

When she came out carrying the empty tray, she saw a fair-haired man leaning against the lintel of the game room, a billiard cue in his hand. From the inside came the click of billiard balls and the sounds of men's voices.

"Why, here's a phantom of beauty," he said in a lifeless tone as she approached. "But if I touched you to see if you were real, it might be misinterpreted." He still leaned exhaustedly against the door frame and looked down a high-bridged nose at her.

"What the devil's run you aground, Grey?" came a voice from inside the room.

The fair-haired man spoke over his shoulder, his gaze fixed on Laura as she passed. "A sweet little sunbeam in the shape of a serving wench."

"All women look the same to him—good. Your shot, Allaire." This voice probably belonged to Nicholas Venner; it sounded silky, deep, and dangerous.

Laura had almost reached the servants' door when the same voice spoke again. "Come back, girl, let's have a look at you."

She retraced her steps, dropping a curtsy and seeing a powerfully muscled gentleman standing in the opening. A pair of insolent gray eyes in an arrogant tanned countenance examined her leisurely, and Laura grew pink with embarrassment.

"New here, I take it. Your name?"

"Laura Adams."

"Your duties?"

"I am here in attendance on Lady Danville."

"Bring ale and three tankards at once," he ordered carelessly, turning to rejoin his friends.

When Laura came back, she saw that the three were playing a desultory game of billiards, and as she set the tray on a side table, the slender man they called Grey approached her, his languid glance fastened on her reddening cheeks.

"A blushing beauty. Egad, Nick, she's a veritable Helen."

"Perhaps like Venus de Milo, beautiful but not all there," commented his host.

Laura made for the door, but Nicholas Venner, straightening from the table, ordered her quietly to stay. "For you know it's quite useless, my girl. Lord Greystan means to have a look at you. Better for Mr. Allaire and me to be present than to meet him in a dark hall, eh, David?" He was looking sardonically at the third gentleman, who had folded his arms and was watching the proceedings imperturbably.

"Yes, of course. You're the damnedest fellow for getting a notion and holding to it buckle and thong, Grey." Mr. Allaire had given Laura a cursory glance while Lord Greystan continued to eye her with an avid look.

"I'll not stay and listen to this," Laura said through set teeth.

Nicholas Venner was regarding her thoughtfully, and he said nothing to stop her as she walked to the door. She could not wait to quit this house and return to Glendon, even though the thought of Lord Danville's infrequent visits home brought with it fear and a kind of trembling excitement.

In the servants' hall she heard later that the two visitors were considered "top-of-the-trees blue bloods", and one of the footmen had the temerity to say of Lord Greystan, "The reason he looks so dog-tired is he don't ever slow down, runs out of harness."

6
CHAPTER

Miss Venner, seated at a writing desk in the morning room, looked up with a fond smile at her brother as he came into the room. He was coatless, his lawn shirt open at the throat below his handsome rakish face.

"Dear Nick," she greeted him, laying down her pen and turning carefully in her chair lest she disarrange her crisp gown of amber muslin. Her face had assumed its little-girl expression.

"Don't trouble to put on that pious aspect, pet. I know all your vices, from the time you began pulling wings from butterflies," he said indifferently, sitting down in a chair and stretching his long legs.

"I don't do that," she protested righteously.

"More fun to do it to people, I suppose, now that you've grown up. That maid of yours, Banks, looks whittled away."

"I merely take her to task when it's necessary," she replied primly.

"I'll warrant you do. What's amazing is that the old man and my mother still don't see through you. Is Danville coming up to scratch?" His look was curious.

"I have hopes," she said shortly.

"Play it carefully and you may snare him. But I'd be careful, Caro, he's as shrewd as he can hold together. Fellow's looked into many a set of beautiful eyes and come away unscathed."

"Do you see him in London as much as formerly?"

"Often. Devilish good company, you know." He smiled lazily.

"Does he—does he speak of me?" Caroline asked with some eagerness.

"No. But he'd not, naturally. And I'll not speak of you to him," he went on significantly. "A rare hobble you'd be in then."

Caroline had the grace to color a little at this. "I would make him a conformable wife," she said defensively.

"Oh, you'd conform all right and tight. Danville would see to that, but he'd have a rude awakening."

"You've gone *your* length many times," said his sister stiffly. "You needn't poker up at *me!*"

Nick laughed. "What a peagoose you are, Caro. Cruelty for cruelty's sake isn't my line—only when it's necessary. But enough of that. I see that you are all proper attention to Lady Danville."

"Yes, she is improving."

"Grey has his eye on her maidservant."

Caroline looked startled. "Laura?"

"The same. Grey needs diversion here in the country."

Caroline sat silent for a moment, and then a slow smile began to form on her full lips. She did not see her brother eyeing her narrowly, nor did she have any inkling of what was in his mind.

"As I recall, your interest in Grey faded some time ago. But I've never seen him more taken with a pretty face; fellow's getting to be a dead bore."

"Why, I had no notion of it. Father has had to reprove Laura."

"In his bad books, eh? I can imagine who put her

there," he remarked sarcastically. "In that case, you won't mind if Grey amuses himself with her."

"It is none of my affair." She shrugged.

"The hitch is that Laura keeps out of sight. Makes it difficult for Grey," he went on.

"Well, I am sure that Mrs. Hedges can employ her around the house. She shares a room with Harris, Lady Danville's dresser," she said meaningfully.

"And what has that to say to the purpose?"

"Harris is jealous of her."

"Wants the girl given a set-down, I take it. You are very helpful." Nick had risen and tweaked one of her raven curls.

"I can't think why you are so concerned about Grey," she offered.

"No, you can't, but you'll smooth the way for him. Can't have the fellow pining away, you know," he said carelessly as he strolled out of the room.

Declaring that he and Mr. Allaire were weary of hearing Lord Greystan harp upon the same string, Nicholas Venner had implied that he would not meddle should that gentleman continue his absurd interest in a mere servant girl. His lordship had declined invitations to accompany the other two, offering such paltry excuses that he wished to explore the church graveyard or that he had a fancy to read a book.

"Don't talk to me of books," Mr. Allaire had rejoined. "I only know cards and men."

"You're becoming obsessed, Grey. We shall all ride to Dorsey and watch the performing bear," urged Nick.

"No such thing. You two go."

"Better sport yet. There's a witch woman in Dolton who can turn herself into a hare—for a sum, of course," his host went on.

Grey evinced a small show of interest. "Why, how's that?"

Nick laughed. "I have not seen it, but it must be so, for she's always followed by a pack of dogs."

"He's more likely looking for a witch with a well-turned ankle," said Mr. Allaire blightingly.

Nick and Allaire had finally taken themselves off, and Lord Greystan was left in the library to look out apathetically onto the formal garden. In a short while he was pleased to see Caroline Venner appear around a corner of the house with Laura in attendance. Miss Venner carried a basket and scissors while Laura followed with a broom and pan. Grey had just stepped out from one of the long windows when he saw that Miss Venner had turned to cutting roses while Laura walked down a path lined with clipped yews. Disappointed at her disappearance, he approached Caroline, his bow languid as usual.

"Why, Grey, you startled me. I thought you gone with the others." Miss Venner's look of surprise seemed genuine.

"Didn't care to," he replied briefly. "Are you setting the servants to sweeping the grass?"

Caroline laughed prettily. "You mean Laura? She is to clean the summerhouse."

"Ah, yes." He inclined his fair head. "Remember it with pleasure. Two summers ago, wasn't it?" he asked slyly.

"I'm sure I don't know to what you refer," she answered stiffly, but he saw the color come and go in her face as she leaned over her basket.

"Daresay you're right; best forgotten," he remarked, his shapely hand slowly rubbing his chin. "Shouldn't have mentioned it . . . unpardonable. Accept my apologies."

"Certainly. I needn't add that you'll keep your tongue between your teeth." Her tone was firm.

"Depend upon it, Caro." He was bowing gracefully.

"It is a fine day. Do take a turn in the garden," she invited graciously as she turned toward the house, her basket full. But she turned back long enough to see him taking the path to the summerhouse.

After attending the fair at Dorsey, Nick and Mr. Allaire rode into the stableyard late in the afternoon. Leaving his host to see to the horses, Mr. Allaire made for the house and did not see the black-clad girl waiting in the shadows.

Laura heard Nicholas Venner's voice directing a groom, and mustered her courage. She needed help, and she could think of no one else in that house who might give it. She felt as if a net tightened on her. The girl had made up her mind to beg Mr. Venner to send her back to Glendon, or failing that, to her father's. She would not try to appeal to Lady Danville, whose recovery might be slowed by worry over her.

Lord Greystan's pursuit of her had grown to such proportions that Laura was afraid. That afternoon he had come upon her in the summerhouse. He had calmly assumed that her dislike of him was nothing but a come-on. Armored in pride, he could not fathom that a woman, especially of her low station, would not welcome his advances.

"You demean yourself and me by your actions, my lord," Laura had told him as he leaned against the door of the summerhouse, blocking the exit.

"Why, here's a pretty moralist," he had sighed. "It only adds to your attractions. I wish to become better acquainted."

"Please excuse me. Besides the impropriety of the thing, I do not desire it."

"Most beauties are damned fatiguing," he observed, ignoring her words. "You're not."

"Let's make an end of this," flared Laura, seeing that reasoning was useless against him. "I was taught virtue and I will hold to it. You were taught the ways of a gentleman; do not fall away from them."

Lord Greystan looked at her in an amazed fashion. "You have a deal of wit and forthrightness beyond your years. Intriguing lass!" And he had advanced, his right hand reaching out for her. The handle of the broom she wielded came down sharply on his wrist, and he had grasped it with his left hand, an incredulous look on his pale handsome features. Laura had sped past him to the door.

Now Laura stepped out to curtsy to Nicholas Venner, his big-muscled frame casting its long shadow on the path.

"What's this?" he inquired abruptly, not in the best of moods.

"I—I would beg a few minutes of your time, sir," she whispered, and he noted the length of the dark lashes resting on her cheeks.

"I am delayed already," he said, his fleshless cheeks and square jaw giving an impression of inflexibility.

"I—I would ask your help, sir," she went on, intimidated even more by his manner.

His large frame relaxed suddenly, and his face was inscrutable as he said slowly, "Laura, isn't it? Well, what's amiss? Out with it."

"It's Lord Greystan," she answered in a subdued tone. "He . . . I do not wish—" She paused.

"You do not wish his attentions. Is that it?"

"Yes," she said roundly.

"To put it baldly, Lord Greystan is a handsome man and seems to be bewitched by you. Are you not curious about the sensation known as love?"

"Love?" Laura had forgotten her fear in indignation. "I want nothing to do with what passes for love in his world."

"You are severe on us, besides being a saucy minx. Lady Danville must have taught you well," he remarked sarcastically.

"She has, as did my mother, sir," replied Laura with such firmness and sweetness in her direct look that his mouth softened in a half-smile.

"Where are your parents?" His lids were narrowed on her with a searching look.

"My mother is dead. My father lives in Dolton in a house owned by Lord Danville."

"So?" And he continued to question her regarding her early history and how she had come to Glendon. Laura answered as evasively and with as few words as possible. However, he evidently saw more in her answers than she intended, for he concluded by remarking sardonically that education had not been squandered on her. Laura had become restless under his persistent questioning.

"And how do you stand with regard to the earl?" Laura grew pale and stood silent. After a long moment he said speculatively, "Not as well as with his mother, I take it. But Danville's a bit high in the instep. Well, as to Lord Greystan, I'll see what can be done."

"Perhaps I could return to Glendon if Lady Danville consents?" she asked eagerly. "But I do not wish her to be troubled about me."

"I'll consider the matter. It won't do to consult Lady Danville," was all that he would say, although he saw that she waited tensely for a positive answer. "Precede me to the house," he ordered coolly, and he followed leisurely, noting how the slanting rays of the sun brightened the heavy coils of her hair.

When Nick encountered his sister in the hall a few moments later, he paused to ask, "How did Grey spend the day? Refused to accompany David and me, as usual."

"Why, he amused himself in the garden, I think. He had it all to himself, except for Laura, who was sweeping out the summerhouse," she informed him with a knowing look.

"Changed my mind, Caro," he said carelessly. "Grey's gotten unreasonable, mad as a weaver. Found a cure for him in the shape of a pretty serving wench at the inn in Dorsey."

Caroline lifted her brows in surprise. "I hope it may work a cure if you wish it." But as he strode off to join his friends in the game room, she sent a summons to Lady Danville's maid to attend her in the morning room.

The summons was promptly answered, even though Harris had been occupied with Lady Danville. Harris had been under Miss Venner's tutelage long enough to give that young lady a blind obedience.

Joining his friends in the game room, Nick was surprised not to find them at billiards. They both lounged in comfortable chairs, a decanter of port at hand. Nick observed that Greystan held his goblet in his left hand, the ruffles at his wrists not quite concealing his bandaged right hand.

"Did you fall, Grey?" he asked gently.

Lord Greystan hastily corrected him. "A rake fell in the stableyard and gave me a blow. Dashed careless of me." He looked carefully at the red glow in his glass.

"Too bad. Shall I send for the doctor?"

"No, no. A mere nothing."

"You'll get nothing out of him, Nick," declared David Allaire. "A trumped-up tale. Wouldn't tell the truth in a diary."

"Veer off, Allaire. Tolerance isn't one of your virtues." Nick frowned. It was a handle that had struck Greystan, he thought cynically as he sat down, but probably not the handle of a rake.

7
CHAPTER

Caroline had sent two letters to Lord Danville; the first expressing her pleasure at his mother's visit, and the second containing the news of her illness. The second letter also spoke of Nick's arrival with his friends, who were also cronies of the earl's. There were a few remarks referring to Laura that could not raise her in his opinion. "Lady Danville brought Harris with her and also a servant girl, Laura. Probably because of her youth, she shows a certain intractability of temper. I have tried to restrain her without upsetting your mother, who is fond of her. However, the gentlemen, especially Lord Greystan, single her out for attention, which has an upsetting effect on the household. In a few years she will no doubt settle into service and prove as valuable a servant as Harris."

On receipt of this missive, Lord Danville, concerned about his mother, hastily canceled an engagement at White's and one with the Duke of Clarence, and set out for Glendon. He arrived in the afternoon and changed horses there, reaching the Venner residence in late afternoon. As he was shown into the hall, Caroline came from the drawing room to meet him, her cameo features lighting up in welcome.

"Forgive my appearance," he greeted her, preoccupied but not forgetting his correct bow. His dark hair was roughened by the wind, and his top boots were dusty.

"Of course, Evelyn," she smiled. "Your mother is improved. You will want to see her at once, I know." She turned to lead him up the broad stairs. As he followed, he noticed that not a ringlet in her glossy hair was out of place. Nor does she talk flowery commonplaces, he thought, vexing a fellow to death with words.

Lady Danville was asleep when they entered, Harris sitting quietly beside her.

"Harris has been untiring," murmured Caroline to him as the maid rose and curtsied. "We will watch now, Harris."

The whispered words caused Lady Danville to stir and to open her eyes. The tears came then when she saw her tall son, and she reached up to caress his cheek as he leaned over her. "I thought you would come."

"Naturally," he said gruffly.

"I'll leave you now and return presently," put in Caroline tactfully, stopping to smooth the counterpane on the bed.

As she left the room, Lady Danville remarked, "She has shown such concern, I could not have been more comfortable at home."

"Caroline is a right one. Now tell me, how soon shall I see you up and about and at home at Glendon?"

"Very soon," she assured him. And her interest in the latest *on-dits* from London that he offered persuaded him that she was right: she would soon be active again. Afraid of tiring her, he soon took his leave, promising to visit her after dinner.

As he rose to go, he paused to ask, "And what of

your maidservant Laura? Has she been attending you?"

"I would not have her in for fear that she would come down with the infection. I have not seen the dear girl since I fell ill, but Caroline assures me that she is kept occupied."

"No doubt," he remarked skeptically. "Perhaps Greystan would like to take on that privilege."

"Why, what do you mean?"

"Well, never mind that," he said pacifically. "Just an idle speculation on my part. You know my propensity to undervalue that girl, and yours to overvalue her."

Later, as he sat with Nick Venner over a tankard of ale, he decided that Caroline's observation that Laura had been an upsetting influence on the household was probably well-founded. Nick confided that the girl had put Greystan in a regular flame, and that Mr. Allaire had lured Grey to the inn at Dorsey, hoping to arouse his interest in a fetching chambermaid there.

"However, it was fruitless," Nick offered lazily. "Grey's monstrously taken with Laura, always hoping to waylay her in a hall or to come upon her in the grounds. Even mumbles about setting the girl up in the world. You know how he is when he takes a notion, goes at it hammer and tongs. No holding him."

His lordship's brows were raised in faint surprise. "What a Jack-pudding. Always a bit hey-go-mad."

"Depend upon it, the fellow's lost to all sense of propriety. She is a lovely little barque of frailty, but a maidservant, after all. Thought you should be apprised of matters."

Danville shrugged his broad shoulders. "It's of no consequence. I hope to remove my mother to Glen-

don in a day or two, and the girl will be absent from
here. Grey puts me in mind of Usher, rigged himself
out in a driving coat with a dozen shoulder capes to
please his light-o'-love."

Nick shuddered. "If that doesn't beat all. Always
did think he lacked perception and sense. Well,
you'll see at dinner Grey's moonstruck look. Allaire's disgusted."

"Can't blame him."

After she had struck Lord Greystan with the broom
handle, Laura had gone in fear of possible consequences, but nothing had happened. She concluded that the gentleman had no wish to advertise
such an experience. He seemed to have forgotten the
incident. She knew now how the fox must feel with
the hounds and huntsmen gaining on him. Somehow
her duties seemed to take her all over the house.
Many of these errands were assigned to her by
Harris, whose secretive air made Laura uneasy. She
hurried through the halls, and before she entered a
room, she gave it a quick survey. Once Lord Greystan had stepped from behind a bookcase in the
library and had insisted on a word with her. She had
curtsied and left without speaking. When she saw
him in a hallway, she retreated and took another
direction. Perhaps Mr. Venner had tried to put a
check on his friend, but Laura had seen no evidence
of it.

Lord Danville's arrival gave her a feeling of relief
as well as the usual disquiet that his presence
brought. Lady Danville was recovering. He would
surely remove his mother to Glendon soon, and
Laura would be away from the hateful attentions of
Lord Greystan and the ill-treatment of Miss Venner.
The girl knew that Miss Caroline would discredit

her to the earl, and she dreaded being in his further disfavor. She longed for an impossible return
to her third-floor captivity in the sewing room at
Glendon.

On the morning after Danville's arrival, Lady
Danville sent word by Harris that Laura should
attend her in the sickroom. After instructions by
Miss Venner to carry out this request, Harris sullen-
ly delivered the message.

When the girl appeared at Lady Danville's bedside, she appeared so overcome that the lady chided
her. "Mercy, child, you look as if *you* have had the
infection!"

"I am so glad you are better," was the tremulous
answer.

"Well, do not pull a long face over it. Has the time
hung heavy?"

"No, ma'am," answered Laura shortly, biting her
lower lip.

"You have been busy, then."

"Yes, my lady."

"Has anyone been unkind to you?" The lady had
not missed the worn look on the girl's lovely face.
After demanding and hearing the facts of the interview with Sir Richard, she looked displeased. She
knew Sir Richard to be stiff-necked, and she liked
neither his part in the incident nor the behavior of
Caroline. Perhaps her notion that Caroline was all
consideration was a mistaken one.

"And what else has happened? Has something else
been plaguing you?" asked the sharp-witted lady,
wanting to hear a full account from the girl.

"It—it is nothing, ma'am, now that we may go
home soon."

"Tell me," she commanded.

"It is of no moment now. I—I seem to have

unwillingly caught the attention of Lord Greystan," she said confusedly.

"So that's it! A good thing I can look after you again." But try as she would, the lady could get no details from the girl. "You are not one to talk, but it is just as I told you—a honey pot, the gentlemen would call you. You are warned now, at any rate, and I am sorry that you had a difficult time."

In the afternoon Laura was ordered by the housekeeper to take a tray of cheese and crusty bread and a bottle of wine to the young master's chambers. She had not seen Lord Danville, and fearing that he had joined Mr. Nicholas there, she knocked hesitantly at the door. Mr. Venner opened the door himself. Laura looked past him anxiously and was relieved to see that he was alone. He had closed the door and leaned his heavy shoulders there, indicating with an imperious gesture that she place the tray on a side table. She turned, expecting to be dismissed, but he stood looking her over with a cool scrutiny from his low-lidded gray eyes. This went on for some time until she shifted her weight uneasily.

"I was just wondering what it is that has driven Greystan up in the boughs. I begin to see some reason in the poor fellow's madness." Laura colored and was silent. "And I begin to think there's something behind that smooth forehead that's not commonly met with. Soon you will have your wish and be well away from his lordship."

"And no thanks to you, sir," she said with some indignation.

He looked rather taken aback. "I made a push to help matters, you know. Mr. Allaire did his best to divert him."

"I know nothing of that, Mr. Venner, but I shall be glad to be gone."

"The earl is ordering carriages to accomplish that in the morning." He saw her face light up. "And do you have such an easy time of it at Glendon that you are so eager to leave here?"

"Not easy, no. I work under Yeats and Mrs. Meers. But I have security and the pleasure of serving Lady Danville."

"You are devoted to the lady."

"I love and admire her," replied the girl simply.

"She is fortunate; gratitude is a scarce commodity. But Greystan will not so easily give up. He intends to stay on and will doubtless visit at Glendon." He had left the door and was decanting the wine.

A dismayed look crossed her heart-shaped face. "I will hope to avoid him," was all that she could say.

He shrugged. "Perhaps you may do so. You may go." And he dismissed her with a curt nod.

But as she traversed the corridor to the kitchen, Laura could not keep from skipping with joy. Tomorrow she would be away from this dreadful house.

The next morning Lord Danville carried his mother to a roomy carriage, and the silent Harris and Laura followed to another. Laura had been passed over while the earl gave Harris instructions for Lady Danville's comfort. She was in his bad books even more, Laura knew intuitively, probably through reports he had heard from Miss Venner and her brother. It would take an Aladdin's lamp to raise her in his good opinion, she thought hopelessly. A smiling Caroline waved good-bye to him from the portico.

8
CHAPTER

They had been at home two days, and Lady Danville had recovered enough strength to be up and about part of the day. The doctor still looked a little severe, but the lady had not scrupled to tell him that he was a grim-faced crape-hanger.

Despite the extra hours spent with Lady Danville, Laura had assumed all her former duties. She hoped to escape a summons from Lord Danville, but it was not to be. On the third morning Yeats majestically informed her that the earl had ordered her to his study. Wordlessly she followed him as he led the way. Lord Danville was seated in the carved chair behind his desk, his dark eyes unreadable as he viewed the slender black-clad figure. She looked down at her hands, her heart making a muffled roar in her ears.

"An explanation is needed, I think, for your pertness and the liberties you took in the Venner household," he said finally.

"I—I tried to please. I hope I was not pert," she got out at last.

"Why, then, does Miss Venner give a poor report of you?"

"I do not know, my lord." She clenched her hands into fists. "She disliked me," she said in a rush.

"I doubt that a feeling of like or dislike crossed her mind," he observed scathingly, making her wish that she had not spoken. "I also hear from Yeats that Harris does not speak well of you, although Mrs. Meers seems to value you."

After quizzing Mrs. Meers that morning, the good woman had defended Laura. "Indeed, my lord, Laura behaves so prudent that we all esteem her—except Harris, that is—she's as jealous as a Barbary pigeon. If the men will let her be, she'll not trouble her pretty self about them." He knew Mrs. Meers to be a woman of sense and was puzzled at the conflicting opinions about Laura. The girl may be just a subtle, artful gypsy, he thought cynically. She should probably be in her father's care, but he could not separate her from his mother, who depended on her.

"Come closer," he now commanded quietly, and she stepped forward reluctantly. "Lord Greystan has called," he informed her. Her pale cheeks suffused with color. "He made excuse to delay in the hall and in the stables. You know the reason. I have warned him off, and I am warning you. These actions must stop."

His words and his mistrust sickened her. She felt like screaming at him with vexation and fear. "I do not need to be warned, my lord. I have despised his attentions. Mr. Venner will tell you that I asked him to settle the matter."

Lord Danville rose and came from behind the desk to stand before her, so overwhelming and with such broad and easily carried shoulders that she felt dwarfed as he towered near her. "If that is so, I shall expect your behavior to conform to those sentiments and to be circumspect in the extreme," he said sternly.

"I—I shall act carefully, my lord. I wish for my lady's and your approval."

"Let me see you earn and merit it, then. Mrs. Meers will be instructed to keep special watch over you." So saying, he nodded dismissal, his eye on her unconsciously alluring figure as she curtsied and left the room.

But despite his warning to Greystan, it was not two days later that he saw him in the park, his horse nibbling the grass nearby. As he saw Danville making for him astride his big gray, he vaulted into the saddle and streaked off; for once in his leisurely life, he hurried.

Lady Danville rested in the afternoons, and it was then that Laura was assigned to domestic tasks by Mrs. Meers and Millie, dusting, polishing, or cleaning silver or brass. There was little time now for reading or reckoning with numbers. At night Laura went to bed worn to a thread.

Millie, knowing that Laura could read, had given her the task of rearranging the books on the library shelves. They needed it badly, Yeats had told her. Laura worked for several days in the library and, with the help of a sliding ladder, had progressed to the higher shelves. She was so absorbed in her work one afternoon that she did not sense as she usually did Lord Danville's quiet entrance. He did not make his presence known, but stood idly leafing through a book.

Laura tidied the books in front of her, and instead of climbing down to move the ladder along, she stretched out to reach the books just along the row. The ladder slipped on the polished floor and she plunged sideways, her head hitting the wood block flooring with a sickening thud. She lay motionless,

stunned and winded. She could not know how swift-
ly he moved, raising and supporting her head.
Finally her lashes fluttered and she opened her eyes.
He looked down into their gentian blankness, concern and even anxiety showing in his own.

Awareness came back to her and a spark ran
through her body at the feel of his hard arm under
her. The warmth of his breath was on her cheek. He
looked at her with a searching gaze, and she dared
not breathe or move. The sparks ran through her
like fire on dry grass in the autumn. She turned her
head away into the fine cloth of his sleeve.

"Th-thank you for catching me," she gasped at
last.

"I was not quick enough," he said huskily.

Laura felt his long-fingered hand slide into her
hair, tracing the lump that was already forming. "It
is nothing," she whispered.

"At best you will have a whacking headache," he
commented, withdrawing his hand and sliding an
arm under her knees. He stood up and carried her to
the door and into the hall. There Yeats stood in his
usual somber dignity.

"The girl has had a fall," he said to him. "Summon
Mrs. Meers to her room and send for the doctor."

Laura felt herself carried easily up the great
staircase and deposited on her bed. His swift glance
circled the little room, seeing its spotless condition
and her small store of books. A few possessions lay
on a shelf, among them a paper fan given her on her
tenth birthday and a bowl of silk flowers that had
been a confirmation present.

Mrs. Meers bustled in, concern on her blunt features. "We'll have her right in a trice, my lord. Tess
is fetching a cold pack for her head."

"Good," he said. "Have the doctor look at the back

of her head, Mrs. Meers, and see that she follows his orders."

"That I will, sir." Mrs. Meers smoothed the hair from Laura's forehead.

Lord Danville stood irresolute, his eyes intently studying the slack figure of the girl. Laura felt a hot flush spreading through her, and she looked back at him with a questioning gaze. His dark brows rose and she shut her eyes. When she opened them, he had quit the room.

The doctor, who visited Lady Danville every day, looked in later. He prescribed powders for the headache, ordered bed rest for a day, and calmly declared that she should be thankful that her foolish action had not given her a cracked skull.

The powders relieved the pain in her head but could not bring sleep until late that night. Laura relived the moments spent with Lord Danville, daring to hope that his disapproval might be abating at last. It seemed to her that in those moments he had softened toward her, but he would have probably shown concern toward any of his servants in a like situation. A kind of panic came over her when she thought of the feelings his touch had aroused in her. He was so unapproachable, so dark and splendid. She still felt the consciousness of being near him. What was this hectic sensation that had come over her? She had not known that feeling could be so sharp and so intense.

Tess carried her meals to her the next day, and Mrs. Meers looked in on her, cheerful as a cricket. "No drawing the bustle for you today, my girl, my lady says. She is dressed and up this morning."

"I am a great deal of trouble to everyone," Laura said ruefully.

"Nonsense! You'll soon be right as rain. His lord-

ship's given orders there's to be no more climbing
that ladder in the library. His secretary is to finish
the job when he comes down from London."

Laura heard these words with a lift of the heart.
Her fall had not been completely forgotten by him.

However, in the following days Lord Danville
seemed to have dismissed her from his mind. It was
almost as if the incident had never happened, except
that she seemed to see him about the house more
frequently. He would walk past her, sometimes
giving her a distant nod but more often ignoring
her.

Once she served tea to him in the library. He was
alone. He sat indolently on the sofa watching her
brew the tea and accepting the cup and cakes from
her hand. In her confusion she awkwardly spilled
tea into the saucer. She expected a sharp set-down,
but he said nothing and waited patiently for her to
fill another.

At unexpected times the earl came to visit his
mother for short periods. The lady's correspondence
had fallen behind, and Laura, at Lady Danville's
dictation, wrote letters for her. His lordship read
some of these, standing near the girl, whose head
was bent over her work.

"This girl seems to do a great deal of scribbling,"
he said idly to his mother, who reclined on a couch
nearby.

"I have a great many letters to answer since my
illness," replied his mother.

"She writes a pretty hand, at any rate," he observed.

"And her spelling and composition are equally as
good." Lady Danville took every opportunity to
praise her charge and was pleased to see that her
difficult son had become more tolerant of Laura.

"But she has been working too hard and has become quite pale."

"Indeed?" He paused and then said, "Instruct Mrs. Meers to decrease her duties somewhat."

But Laura felt that any ground she may have gained with him was lost the next day. She had again ascended a short ladder in the morning room. The smaller candelabra mounted on the walls were the responsibility of the maids, and she was replacing the spent candles with new ones. She felt the ladder tremble under her, and she looked down to see two powerful hands steadying it and to hear a crisp command to come down. Laura hastily descended into the circle made by two strong arms. Lord Danville had not removed his hands, and she felt the warmth of him there behind her, his breath in her hair. Her heart began its now-familiar thumping. She could not turn around. She was held prisoner there for a moment that seemed an hour, and then he stepped back.

"About-face, please. You were told not to climb ladders," he grated.

Laura turned toward him; one glance showed his thinned lips and a line between the black brows. "That was in the library—I mean, I . . . this ladder is shorter."

"And what has that to say to anything?"

She opened her mouth to speak, and another glance at his hard countenance caused her to change her mind.

"I thought I had seen signs that you are endeavoring to suppress your contrary nature; I was mistaken." His voice was tinged with ice. "I presume that you have a proper sense of obligation to the family you serve here?" he went on, his eyes on her in a suddenly still and passionless look.

"Yes, my lord." Her lower lip trembled so that she was obliged to catch it between her teeth.

"You need not trouble to put on that grievous look," he said calmly, and his hand came up to take her lightly by her rounded chin, his thumb firm against her jawline. She was completely and acutely aware of his touch in every nerve. His critical gaze examined her as coolly as if she had been a painting on the wall, noting the rose-petal skin and her eyes like blue lakes.

"There's some reason for Greystan's addled wits, no doubt." He withdrew his hand and stood for a moment watching the hot color stain her cheeks. She glanced up to see a flicker of a smile disappearing on his face. "Have a care what you are about," he then ordered. "The footmen may assume this duty hereafter." His gesture indicated the wall sconces as he turned toward the door.

But when he had gone, Laura stood for several seconds in a trance. All of a sudden her senses heightened: the light from the window was brighter, sounds were sharper, her body felt as light as the breeze that stirred the draperies. She shook her muddled head. Maybe the fall had affected her, but she must concentrate on the task at hand. She could not bear to think of what consequences another blunder would bring down on her head.

9
CHAPTER

One sunny afternoon Laura sat at Lady Danville's bedside. It seemed that her lady was feebler and that she slept more each day. From the window the meadows beyond were beautiful in their early-summer colors of green and yellow.

"How rich the colors are in the sun," commented Lady Danville—almost as if she knew that she might not see that scene again, thought Laura with a pang.

"Pray bring me the black enameled box on the dressing table," she asked, and Laura obediently placed it in her hands. From it Lady Danville drew out a heavily carved silver pendant cross on a chain and a small leather purse.

"I have meant to give you this crucifix for a long time, my dear, and I have here eight gold guineas meant for your father. He is to keep them against a time of need."

Laura protested that her ladyship had already indulged her too often and that her father would think the same, but Lady Danville would not be denied. "Too few people realize that the giver has the greater joy," she declared. "Now sing me something sleep-provoking, lass."

And so Laura sang to her over and over a fifteenth-century lullaby, until the lady fell asleep.

A woman is a worthy thyng
They do the wash and do the wrynge,
'Lullay, Lullay! she doth synge,
And yet she has but care and woe.

All unconscious she sang, unaware of the sadness that had crept in or that anyone heard the low tone. She was thinking that with Lady Danville she had always had a feeling of belonging. It was she who had given her, Laura, the tools with which to think and the opportunity to enrich her mind.

Laura did not know that Lord Danville had come into the adjoining sitting room and that he stood motionless there. When her singing faded away, he stepped to the doorway and beckoned her into the room. She dipped him a curtsy as he leaned against a center table. He was coatless, his fine shirt open at the neck, showing the smooth brown column of his throat.

"It is well that you are able to please and soothe my mother," he said in a low tone. "How does she go on?"

"She—she does not complain, my lord."

"I would not expect it. Does she gain strength?"

"She does not recover her usual energy, sir," replied Laura hesitantly.

He frowned and rose to stand at the window, tall and lean, the breadth of his shoulders blocking out the light. "What have you in your hand?" he asked, his back to her.

Laura looked down bemusedly at her hand. "Why, a pendant my lady gave me and monies she gave me for my father's care."

"Your father's name?"

"James Adams, sir. He lives in Dolton."

"I am aware of that," he said absently, his mind on

something else. Suddenly he wheeled toward her impatiently. "Return to your lady's bedside," he snapped, startling her.

She looked at him helplessly for an instant, gave her small bob of a curtsy, and fled back to the bedroom. He cannot bear even the sight of me, she thought miserably.

Laura sat quietly for some time at Lady Danville's side and had supposed that the earl had left the sitting room. She was surprised to hear his voice in the next room, and she recognized the answering voice. It was Miss Venner. That young lady called regularly, and on the days she did not come, a nosegay of flowers or a basket of fruit was delivered.

The two in the next room talked for a while in low tones, but Laura did not hear what was said. Then she realized that they had approached the connecting door, for their voices became audible to her.

"Is Harris attending her?"

"She is asleep. Laura is with her."

"I have the highest opinion of Harris; experience has made her so much more capable than Laura."

"In a practical way you may be right. But Laura has become my mother's doting piece."

"I had heard that, and knowing the girl as I do, I knew that you could not be pleased."

"I am persuaded that she is deeply attached to my mother, and that must please me."

They came into the room. Caroline, looking entrancing in a gown of paisley print, gave Laura a look that wished her at the bottom of the Red Sea. The earl, who followed her, nodded a dismissal, and Laura thankfully made her exit.

Lady Danville was getting no better. That she was well-loved was easily seen in the muffled footsteps and voices of the servants and in their eagerness to please. The knocker sounded often, but the lady was not well enough to receive many visitors.

Laura was relieved of her domestic duties, and either she or Harris was always with her ladyship. The doctor described her ailment as respiratory failure and palpitations of the heart, and bluntly told the earl there was no hope of recovery. Laura slept on a bed in Lady Danville's dressing room, alert even in her sleep for any sound from the next room.

But Lady Danville rarely uttered a repining word, although she must often have been in the greatest discomfort. Her patience, resignation, and good humor were extraordinary.

The earl made short visits to her bedside. He knew that lengthy conversation tired her but that the sight of him cheered her. She began to speak of her passing, to which she seemed perfectly resigned. Her only worry was for those she would leave behind, and she laid on her son instructions and bequests for friends, tenants, villagers, and servants. He ordered Laura to keep a record of these so that none would be forgotten or overlooked.

Many times Lady Danville asked that she and her son be alone, and on one such occasion she spoke to him about Laura.

"I hope you will be a protector to Laura, as well as to all the servants, for we owe them protection as much as a king owes it to his subjects."

"Do not concern yourself. I have come to think better of her after seeing so much innocence in her behavior."

"It is as I told you, Evelyn, her sense and judgment so far surpass her years and the opportunities she has had." She went on with a significant look. "But it is no surprise to me."

Her son directed an inquiring look at her.

"I fear for her in her innocence and low estate. I have not been at liberty to speak freely about Laura, but the time has come for me to do so."

Talking was very difficult for her, he saw. He leaned over to caress her cheek. "Be easy, Mama. When you have rested, we will speak more about this. I will be back directly."

It was late that same night that Lady Danville's breathing became labored, and she passed into an unconscious state. Lord Danville and the doctor were with her, and toward morning she expired without regaining consciousness.

Her son sat alone with her for some time, and the doctor descended the stairs with orders to Yeats that he see to the placing of the hatchment, a panel bearing the Danville coat of arms, over the door and the tying of the knocker with crape. He also sent for Mrs. Meers and suggested that she save his lordship as much as possible by seeing to the laying out. He himself would order a casket sent from Dolton that might properly be placed in the large parlor. As an afterthought the sensible man cautioned Yeats to send for extra carriages, as the funeral cortege was sure to be a long one. With that, he took himself off.

In the following days Laura, feeling as if she was made of wood, did what was required of her. Mrs. Meers declared that she was not to mope herself to ribbons. "Adone do! My lady wouldn't wish it, and there's a jam-up of work to be done, what with the funeral meats to be got ready and the knocker never still."

When Lady Danville had been laid in the parlor, a

procession of people came to show respect, from the humblest person to the Duke of Clarence, who came as proxy for his royal brother. The line continued for two days, as Lady Danville had been loved by the villagers as well as by the rich and titled, who came in elegant carriages drawn by black-plumed horses.

The funeral was at noon on the third day, the cortege setting out from Glendon. Alone in the first carriage was Lord Danville, followed by the carriages of relatives and friends. At the end of the procession were the household servants in plain carriages and humbler persons, many on foot. The Countess of Danville was carried to the church in Dolton, which she had endowed, and was buried in the churchyard in a vault under a monument of black marble. The service was brief. A cold collation was provided at Glendon for the chief mourners, who returned there after the interment.

The days seemed endless to Laura, but Mrs. Meers' bracing common sense kept her from giving way to grief. She kept Laura fetching and carrying so that she had no time for tears. Many of the mourners lingered for several days, some staying at the house and others sleeping at the inns in Dorsey and Dolton.

Laura caught only glimpses of Lord Danville, his countenance marked by an increased austerity and reserve. Lady Venner and Caroline, suitably clad in somber raiment, were ever-present, and Harris, her eyes red from weeping, announced to Laura, "Miss Caroline will be the next countess before the year's out, mark my words, and then ye'll be pulled off your high perch!"

At the time of the funeral, Pax, the old house dog, disappeared. In the instinctive way of animals, he must have sensed what had happened. With many of

the servants away, he had found it easy to slip out.
The earl ordered a search for him, but no one had
seen the dog after the funeral. Laura worried about
him, picturing him lying hungry and thirsty under
a bush, too weak to find his way home. With Mrs.
Meers' permission, she went out hunting for him.

She made her way through the home wood and
followed the creek as it twisted and turned. At
intervals she called the dog's name, pushing
through thickets looking for him. The day darkened
and it began to drizzle. Her face was wet with rain.
She wore an old blue cloak and a knitted cap of red
wool pulled down over her ears. Beneath it tendrils
of soft hair turned outward in disarray. She looked
like a little girl meant for simple childish pleasures.

Past a bend in the creek she heard the nicker of a
horse, and into her view rode the earl astride a
powerful black, his damp coat molded like a second
skin to his wide shoulders. But Laura's eyes were
drawn to what lay across his saddle. It was Pax, stiff
in death. Over the horse's head Laura met the
bleakness of dark eyes in a countenance taut with
fatigue.

Grief took Laura by the throat. She had repressed
it for days. She did not cry out or make a sound, but
the muscles of her face contracted and tears gushed
from her closed eyelids. Her hands kneaded desperately one against the other.

"You were looking for Pax?" His voice was tired.

"Yes, my lord," she said tremulously, her face
screwed up like a young child's.

"You grieve for Pax and my mother. It was the
dog's time. He went away to die."

"Yes," she said, choking back a sob.

"You are wet and have wandered too far away
from the house. I will follow as you return." She

looked up at him, not comprehending for an instant. The hard outline of his mouth took on a gentler curve and the arrogant dark gaze softened. "Tell Mrs. Meers to prepare you a brandy posset and put you to bed."

Laura nodded, still crying helplessly, and hurried to retrace her steps, aware that he swung his horse toward her and waited patiently to follow.

The last mourner finally departed, and relief was plain on the faces of the overworked servants. Laura helped Mrs. Meers to gather the garments and personal effects of Lady Danville, some of it to be stored but more to be given away according to her bequests. Caroline was delighted to receive two bolts of embroidered French silks and an ermine wrap. Mrs. Meers was overcome when his lordship handed her ten gold pieces and a pearl ring of antique design.

Lord Danville had been occupied with settling the details of his mother's estate. One afternoon he summoned Laura to come to his study. When she appeared, he was not behind his desk, but stood braced with an elbow against the carved mantel, a contemplative look on his dark countenance. He turned at her entrance to look at her measuringly. Laura's pulse sped.

"Had your mistress made any dispensation to you before she died?"

"Yes, my lord. She gave me a silver crucifix and money to be given to my father," she answered, relief flooding through her that she was not to receive one of his set-downs.

"She wished your father to be cared for. He may continue to live in the cottage she provided for him."

"My father will be pleased, sir."

"How does he go on?"

"I—I have been able to see him only twice lately. He is well enough, Mrs. Moffitt says."

"Who is she, pray?"

"She looks in on my father and brings him meals," replied the girl nervously.

"You may now resume your regular visits to him," he instructed, removing his elbow from the mantel and picking up from there a small reliquary box and a chain. "This box contains five gold pieces, a further gift for your father. I wish you to have this gold chain of my mother's, you will see that it is intricately carved and quite old." He motioned her forward, and Laura's breath grew tight at this unfamiliar sensation of being close to him. As she took the gifts from his palm, she started at the vibration that traveled up her arm and lodged in the region near her heart.

"Th-thank you, my lord." She stepped back a pace, her cheeks as red as poppies.

His eyes narrowed. "I am aware that you write a pretty script and that you understand the niceties of language. In the absence of my secretary, who must unavoidably remain in London, I shall make use of those talents." She looked up to see a trace of a smile on his handsome features. "Come, I will show you the considerable paperwork that needs doing."

He stepped past her to a door leading into a small paneled room off the study. On a desk in the center of the room were several piles of letters, easily five hundred or more.

"These are letters of condolence. You may undertake to acknowledge as many as do not need a personal answer—I leave that to your judgment. Two or three hours of application every afternoon should soon see them diminished. Compose the

usual answer to letters of this kind; acknowledg-
ment of receipt, appreciation for the writer's concern. You will find proper notepaper in the drawer."
He stood waiting for an answer from her, but none
came. "Well, have you a bone in your throat that you
cannot answer?"

Laura cleared her throat as if she did indeed have
a bone in it. "I will do my best," she finally got out.

"Mrs. Meers is to release you from afternoon
work. You may begin tomorrow." His black head
nodded dismissal, and Laura made her obeisance.

Mrs. Meers was taken aback when Laura told her
of her new responsibility. "I do declare. I'd as soon
expect to see a pig in church as to see his lordship
making a secretary of a little lass like you."

Laura smiled faintly and anxiously resolved to
stay up late composing letters and practicing pen-
manship.

The next afternoon Yeats informed her that the
master was away but that she might begin her new
assignment. She sat gingerly at the desk and began
to sort the letters, placing those in a separate pile
that she thought Lord Danville might prefer to
answer himself. She was well into this task when
she felt the focus of his eyes on her, although he had
made no sound. She turned hastily. He stood tall in
the entrance, the suggestion of humor on his lean
countenance making him look dangerously attractive. Laura rose to her feet.

"Continue as you were," he said easily. "You will
never finish if you are forever bobbing up at my
entrance." He came to stand by the desk as Laura,
her breath quickening at his nearness, reseated
herself. "You have the sorting well started, I see.
Place those that I should answer on my desk in the
study. Perhaps you have done enough for today."

"I am not tired, sir," murmured Laura.

"As you will." He shrugged. She heard his receding footsteps and his voice speaking to Yeats in the hall.

After a few days Laura decided that his lordship found her work acceptable, as he made only a casual suggestion here and there. When he was in his study, his near presence caused her concentration to waver. Through the closed door as he talked to others, and although she could not distinguish the words, she came to know every cadence in his voice; from approbation to displeasure, from calmness to anger, from gravity to laughter. She could never hear that voice without being acutely aware of it.

One afternoon she was told that it was a hunt day and that his lordship was absent. It was a good day to finish the job, she thought. She worked until almost dusk, finally finishing the last letter and laying down her pen with a sigh. Her fingers were cramped from writing and she was missing her tea. As she quietly opened the door into the study, she saw two figures standing in the hall just beyond the study door.

Laura's heart turned over as if to smother her. It was Caroline Venner and Lord Danville. As if in slow motion she saw his ruby-coated arm reach out. He raised Caroline's chin, standing over her and looking down into her upraised face. Then his dark profile descended and his lips brushed hers for an instant. He released Caroline then and turned his back, concealing his companion.

Time stopped for Laura. She could not move, could hear only the deep and slow tone of his voice as he addressed Caroline. Then the figures disappeared from her view, and she heard the outside door closing on them.

Consciousness returned. She made for the door and forced her trembling limbs to carry her up the broad stairs, her hand gripping the rail. She had known that Lord Danville favored Caroline Venner, but this proof that there was real attachment between them hit her like a thunderbolt. It was somehow unbelievable. She had to be alone to comprehend it.

When she came to her room, she sat hunched down on the bed, her arms over her head as if she were trying to hide. The thought of that dark urbane countenance bending over the flowerlike face of Caroline was like a knife in her side. The day that she comes to Glendon as a bride will be a fearful one for me, thought Laura; I cannot bear to stay here even if she would allow it. Despair gripped her as futile tears squeezed from under her lids.

Mrs. Meers cheerfully declared that Laura was blue-deviled because she must come back now to scrubbing and cleaning. After all, she reasoned, it was enough to overset anyone to be a brain-box one day and a parlormaid the next. Laura's sunny smile returned, but it was not as spontaneous as before. Her sensitive mouth had a new look of resolution and a hint of melancholy in its curve.

It was the earl himself who caused her spirits to revive. He came upon her in the library as she stood for a moment, dust cloth in hand, admiring two newly hung illustrations of birds.

"Do you know those birds?" he asked casually. He had just come in, and Laura turned a flustered face toward him.

"The one, my lord," she said awkwardly, indicating the lapwing, "but I do not know its name."

"A part of your education neglected by my mother," he remarked sardonically. "It is a lapwing, and the other is a sand martin. Did not my mother give into your hand *White's Natural History?* It is a classic, full of new discoveries. He was devoted to descriptions of songbirds and game birds."

"No, sir."

"You shall look into it," he stated, turning on his booted heel to take the book from the shelves. "What is it, Yeats?" he asked of the butler, whose severe countenance had appeared in the doorway.

"Nothing, my lord—that is, I came to overlook Laura's work."

"She is occupied, as you can see," he said coolly, and Yeats hastily took himself off. The earl returned, laying the book on the table and seating himself in a chair, the hard muscles in his legs displayed to advantage in tight fawn-colored breeches. "Those prints are by Bewick of Newcastle, a great illustrator of birds. Having spent your life in the country, you can no doubt learn to attach names to the birds you have seen from childhood."

"Yes, my lord. I—I have had pleasure in watching them," she said hesitantly, twisting the dust cloth behind her back. She could not believe that he would condescend to speak to her in this manner.

"Naturalists are beginning to come out of doors and look at this proud island," he said then, going on to speak about such matters as a balance in nature and the need to know the quiet and untrodden silence. As he talked, Laura lost herself in his words, and she thought of a line that she had learned from Blake.

> Kill not the moth nor butterfly
> For the Last Judgment draweth nigh.

Of a sudden the earl seemed to recollect himself. "Proceed with what you were doing," he ordered, his

hooded gaze on her soft mouth. Laura came out of
her woolgathering and turned guiltily to her dusting. His dark gaze on her, she reached up to wipe the
mantel, her raised arms pulling tight the bodice of
her gown and revealing the lovely young curves of
her figure.

"Take the book when you go. Mrs. Meers is to
allow you to look into it," he instructed, rising from
his chair and abruptly striding from the room.

10
CHAPTER

Surprisingly, Nicholas Venner prolonged his visit to the country, even though his two friends had returned to the pleasures of town life. His father, Sir Richard, so frequently expressed his delight at the extended visit that his son finally declared it past bearing. He dampeningly informed his parent that unless he refrained from such unseemly displays of affection, he, Nick, would take off for London the next day.

"You should not be so severe on Papa," his sister had reproved him privately.

Her brother raised his eyebrows in some surprise. "The fellow gets to be a dashed nuisance, forever rubbing his hands with glee. But never mind that. How goes it with Danville? I saw that you were in high force during the funeral festivities."

A complacent look settled on Caroline's face. "I believe that he begins to depend upon me."

"I daresay. But that don't mean he'll propose. I confess to a liking for him; Danville's top of the trees. Greystan's a fool to have forfeited his friendship over that slip of a maidservant."

"It was ridiculous, his hanging about at Glendon and receiving such a set-down from Evelyn."

Nick looked amused. "Allaire writes that Grey's still not over his infatuation. Down in the dumps and wasting the ready at the gaming tables. Allaire's tolerably certain he'll be back here within the month to try his hand again with the girl."

"I cannot see the attraction. She's a forward minx and nothing above the ordinary."

"I am well aware that you'd do her a mischief if you could, little sister. If Greystan whisked her away, you'd not wear the willow."

"Well, of course not. Harris tells me that the little slut has been set to writing in a room off the study and that Mrs. Meers makes a great pet of her."

Nick laughed. "I see it all. I'd lay a monkey Harris will be the new housekeeper at Glendon if Danville comes up to snuff."

"I have already thought of that," replied Caroline, pressing her full lips tightly together. "Harris tells me that the old vicar from Dolton has been called in. She suspects that he might be given the task of tutoring the wench further."

"What the Hades!" exclaimed Nick in astonishment. "I strongly doubt it. Danville's too much a man of sense for that."

"You would think so," agreed Caroline grimly. "Devil take the hussy!"

This was said with such a look of venom that her brother was moved to comment, "I'd wipe that look off if I were you, Caro. It's hardly becoming."

But Harris suspicion was correct that Mr. Gaunt, who had lived in seclusion in Dolton for ten years since his retirement, had been delegated to oversee Laura's further education. By temperament a scholar, he had formerly been the vicar in Dolton, and the appointment had not been a happy one. Mr. Gaunt had had little patience for weaknesses of the flesh and the follies of his flock. He had been happier in his retirement, cultivating the wits of certain chosen sons of the neighboring gentry who showed intellectual promise. Often tired of trivial conversation, the earl had frequently sought his company, fully appreciating his flashes of subtle wit and his original views on controversial subjects. He once confided to his mother that an evening of rational conversation with Mr. Gaunt was worth ten spent in idle talk at White's or at a rout.

"To me he lacks that most important attribute, tolerance toward his fellow human beings," she had replied with a severity unusual in her.

Laura knew of Mr. Gaunt, as did every person in and around Dolton. She had not been told, however, that this arbitrary and highly intelligent old gentleman was to become her mentor. Early one morning she was ordered to the study and found the earl behind his work-strewn desk. He looked up at her entrance, his abstracted gaze relieving her anxiety. Perhaps he is not vexed after all, she thought, unclenching her hands behind her back.

"Advance closer, please," he instructed, laying down his pen and leaning back in his chair. "I have taken a decision regarding your further education," he announced abruptly.

Laura's blue eyes opened wide in surprise. "Y-yes, my lord," she said confusedly.

"You need not look saucer-eyed," he reproved. "I was well pleased with the manner in which you answered the letters. My mother's estimate of your ability appears to have been correct."

This word of praise was so gratifying to Laura that she grew red as fire, and she closed her eyes for an instant.

"I presume you know Mr. Gaunt, the former vicar, at least by reputation. The worthy gentleman shall take up where my mother's schooling left off." Laura was looking at him in stupefaction, and she heard the deep sound of his sudden laugh. "You must not look so bewildered, else I must revise my good opinion of your talents."

Laura plucked up her spirit at last. "Well, sir, it is such an about-face."

"A thinking man—and I aspire to be one—should be able to change his mind. I wish to honor my mother's hopes for you. There are other reasons also, which cannot be told here."

"I—I do not know what to say, my lord."

"You need say nothing, only apply yourself to the difficult course Mr. Gaunt will no doubt lay out for you."

"I promise to do so."

"That is well. Mr. Gaunt will begin on Monday, coming here three mornings a week. He will evaluate the advances you have already made and will thereafter give me a weekly progress report."

So appalling was the last part of this remark that Laura was filled with dread. She had heard of the short shrift Mr. Gaunt made of backward pupils.

"I can have no hope of pleasing such a high stickler as I know Mr. Gaunt to be. He will no doubt label me a numskull."

"Have no fears on that score. It is true that he is not overly pleased to take on a member of your sex; he is used to dealing only with promising young men. However, I have acquainted him with some of your history, and he agrees to give you a fair trial. Proper respect and diligent application on your part should serve to appease his sometimes unreliable disposition. Remember that the best teacher usually demands more than his pupils can achieve." This was said firmly but not unkindly.

Laura felt as if she had plunged into water over

her head. "I am eager to learn as much as I am able, my lord, but I feel too ignorant to meet Mr. Gaunt's high standards."

"There is no knowing until one makes the effort, is there? I shall expect to hear from him that you apply yourself earnestly." His expression demanded compliance, and under that gaze Laura could not speak. She curtsied silently.

"I expect you to spare no effort to please him." His tone was inflexible.

Laura knew better than to protest further. "Yes, sir."

"Good. Your duties will be considerably lightened so that you have time for study. I believe that takes care of the matter." His hand had taken up one of the papers on the desk and he took no further notice of her. Laura felt herself dismissed.

When Harris was told that she was assigned to many of Laura's chores, the maid's cup of bitterness was full. Since Lady Danville's death, her influence in the house had lessened, and having to assume the duties of a parlormaid was a comedown. Her only comfort was that Miss Venner sympathized with all these confidences and assured her that the time might come when the tables were turned. Harris might hasten that day as long as she kept her counsel. Miss Venner even suggested that Harris' new duties gave her a better opportunity to know what went on at Glendon.

Mrs. Meers was ordered to ready the schoolroom, which was in the back part of the house on the second floor. The master's desk stood on a raised platform at one end. Along the farther wall ran a blackboard. Two large windows at the back of the room gave light.

Laura peeked in to see that her books and painting supplies had been brought from storage and were on a table near the center of the room, along with a good supply of paper and quill pens. Her desk, with an attached writing board, stood near the table. The sight of the room caused her stomach to curl with apprehension, and when Monday came, she approached the door as if she entered a lion's den.

Mr. Gaunt sat erect at the master's desk engaged in placing bookmarks in several volumes. Bushy white eyebrows added to the harshness of his expression, and when he glanced up, she saw that his eyes were of that pale-blue color that can so easily freeze with a glance.

"Have you no schoolroom manners, miss?" His voice was low, his diction perfect, and his tone curt.

"The village school is the only one I have attended, sir," replied Laura, determined to hide her fear and put on a brave face before this man of learning.

"The student stands at the door and makes an obeisance until directed further," he said icily, his eyes again on his task.

Laura curtsied respectfully.

After several moments, Mr. Gaunt indicated the books on his desk. "After I have judged either the level of your achievement or the depth of your ignorance, we can begin to delve into these volumes. You may take them and be seated." When Laura was seated stiffly at her desk, he went on. "When I question you or require a recitation, you will ordinarily stand beside the desk, but as today's session will largely be a matter of my quizzing you, you may sit with your hands folded before you."

Laura felt that she would not be able to find an answer even to the simplest question.

At the end of the first half-hour of queries—

ranging from ordinary arithmetic, of which Laura had a fair knowledge, to elementary algebra, about which she knew nothing—he sat back in disgust.

"A typically female mind, which cannot understand even the simplest ciphering. If you are as deficient in other fields as you are in numbering, I shall have to declare to the earl that I find you unteachable."

This appalling threat put a spur to Laura's courage. She burst out, her eyes fixed on her tightly folded hands. "And you would be quite mistaken, sir. Lady Danville found me teachable, but she did not petrify me or set me to quaking as you do." Here she looked directly at him, to see his white eyebrows raised in disbelief.

"Well! I finally get a round answer. I had almost decided that what you lacked in intelligence you made up for in stupidity. You do not have a block for a head, after all. Do you know anything at all about numbering?"

"I know arithmetic but nothing of higher mathematics."

"And what do you have to say of your knowledge in general?"

"There are great gaps missing, but I have tried to comprehend the books Lady Danville set me to read. I hope that I write legibly and clearly. I have enough wit to know that if I study for a decade, I shall still be a novice in learning."

"You encourage me," he said abruptly. "That is a truth that many learned fools never realize."

So the schooling began, and Laura soon gained confidence after she detected an occasional glint of humor in Mr. Gaunt's cold blue eye. He was a high stickler, however, and many a candle guttered in its socket as she studied late into the night. In the first

few weeks of this routine she saw nothing of the
earl; he spent a great deal of time following the
hounds, often at the Duke of Charlesworth's hunting seat near Dorsey, the next village.

Laura did not know that Mr. Gaunt was surprised
at her progress; he had decided that her mind
resembled a blotter. Her ability to retain facts and
subsequently use those facts as tools for reasoning
he had thought to be only a masculine trait. The old
gentleman took care not to show his surprise lest his
pupil relax her efforts.

Laura's comprehension of the French language
had improved, but Mr. Gaunt, dissatisfied with her
expression and enunciation, assigned for memoriza-
tion a long passage from Rousseau's *La nouvelle
Héloïse*. For several days she had been required to
recite it and was frequently interrupted and corrected.

"You may repeat the passage again today," Mr.
Gaunt decreed. "Should your diction still require
frequent interruption, you shall commit to memory
an extensive passage from the *Maximes* of La Rochefoucauld. That threat should cause you to recite
carefully today, mademoiselle." Mr. Gaunt's eyes
had traveled to the door, where the tall figure of
Lord Danville lounged in the opening with folded
arms. Unseen by Laura, he signed to the tutor to
continue. "Stand and begin, ma'am."

Anxious to avoid the possible heavy assignment,
Laura began fifteen minutes of slow and careful
recitation, her eyes fixed in concentration. Her
teacher did not interrupt.

"Bravo!" said a well-remembered voice from the
door, and Laura jumped with apprehension. But
Lord Danville's dark eyes gave her only a cursory
glance as he spoke to Mr. Gaunt. "But perhaps it is

not advisable for one in her position to acquire notions above her station. Is that not the theme, the humble hero who rises in an aristocratic society?"

"It is, my lord. She was assigned it not so much for the context as for an exercise to improve her diction."

"Well, enough, I daresay it accomplished its purpose." And he advanced into the room to take up a discussion with Mr. Gaunt on a fairly recent novel, *La Religieuse,* which Danville held to be untidily and carelessly written. Laura, ignored by both of them, remained standing.

Recollecting himself at last, the earl glanced at Laura. "But I interrupt the lesson. Your pupil continues to improve, Mr. Gaunt?"

"Her progress is faster than I had expected, sir." Her tutor looked at her with a faint smile.

"I trust you will see to it that she goes on at a smart pace. Besides keeping her well occupied, she learns restraint and discipline." Laura thought the same might be said of a mettlesome horse, but she took care that no such feeling showed in her expression.

"In that case I shall assign the passage from La Rochefoucauld; it is certain to keep wayward thoughts away from the mind."

"By all means," replied the earl carelessly as he strolled to the door.

As Laura began to memorize the difficult French passage that evening, she devoutly hoped that the earl would not come to the schoolroom often. The result of his visit was an increase in her already heavy assignments. And he would hear from Mr. Gaunt if she failed to come up to the mark, she thought apprehensively. She bit her lip as she thought of being summoned before the earl because of a complaint from Mr. Gaunt. She could almost feel his presence like a dark shadow, his cold gaze pinning her like a butterfly. Laura felt a shiver run down her back and she wriggled uncomfortably. She must make a good start on memorizing the long passage tonight and then write an analysis of Malory's *Morte d'Arthur,* which she had yet to finish reading. She stretched her spine and neck, and her tired head bent again over her books.

11
CHAPTER

In the morning Mrs. Meers shook her head at the girl's wan appearance. "Ye'll find yourself laid by the heels in bed effen you keep hammering at those books till the cock crows."

"But it keeps me from having wayward thoughts," Laura replied. "I am well enough, Mrs. Meers."

The housekeeper said no more but silently determined to mention the matter to the earl.

"The poor girl works double hours and without letup," she explained to Lord Danville as he rose from the breakfast table. "She don't get out in the air 'cept to see her father on Fridays. There be something taking abut Laura, my lord, and begging your pardon, I plucked up my spirit to speak to you."

His lordship's expression was indifferent. "Commendable of you, Mrs. Meers. Has Laura complained?"

"That she has not, sir, nary a squeak."

"Say no more, the matter will be looked into." He turned to leave the room but paused at the door. "When Laura goes to Dolton on Fridays, does she go alone?"

"One of the grooms drives her in the gig, my lord."

"She is never to go beyond the estate or to Dolton unattended," he said shortly, his gaze intent.

Mrs. Meers followed him with a puzzled look as he left the room. She knew of Lord Greystan's past interest in Laura, but he had only been visiting in the neighborhood then and she strongly doubted that he was a threat now. The master might be making a piece of work about nothing. That evening she was surprised to learn from the impassive Yeats that Lord Greystan was again a guest at the Venner residence.

"Well, if that don't beat all," observed the good woman. "I wouldn't say he'd be welcome there after making such a cake of himself over Laura, even chasing after her here at Glendon. The master don't like it above half, I can tell you."

"I am aware of all that, Mrs. Meers," replied Yeats loftily. "It is not our place to question who stays at the Venner residence."

"That's as may be," affirmed Mrs. Meers stoutly. "But mark my words, they don't invite him just for the pleasure of his company. Miss Caroline has a hand in it, whatever it is."

"I repeat, we do not criticize our betters, Mrs. Meers. After all, Miss Venner will likely be the future mistress of us all one day."

"And likely to show Laura and me the back door the same day," returned Mrs. Meers, thrown into a gloom by Yeats' remark.

After several exhausting nights, Laura had almost mastered her memory work, but she hoped that Mr. Gaunt would allow a little more time for it to become rote. As she prepared to visit her father that afternoon, she reflected that she was actually becoming fond of her tutor; his sternness was often softened now by a humorous or kindly gleam from his pale-blue eyes.

A groom awaited her in the gig, and as Laura came out the back door laden with a basket and a holdall containing her father's newly laundered clothing, the groom sprang down to assist her. At that moment, the earl, clad in riding attire, appeared from the direction of the stables. His eye fell on them, and making a sign to the groom to stand by, he approached.

Laura, flustered by the sight of him, stood holding the basket, the breeze loosening tendrils of her tightly coiled hair and lifting her skirts to show a pair of dainty ankles.

"What have you in the basket that you hug it so closely?" he asked, his crop making a careless tattoo against his booted leg.

The groom guided the gig to the end of the lane.

"A leg of mutton and fruit and pudding, sir. Mrs. Meers knows of it."

"Your manner suggests that you have pilfered the silver as well." He smiled a slow smile, showing the edge of his white teeth.

Encouraged by that smile, she replied, "You may search it if you wish, sir."

"A sauce-box. You have set out to visit your father, I see."

"Yes." She glanced up, conscious only of the mad hammering of her heart.

"Who gave you those unfairly beautiful eyes?" His fingers came up to trace the crescents of her brows. She held her breath. One instant passed, then two, then three. Suddenly self-derision pulled at his lower lip, and his hand fell. "And also that look of innocence?" he asked scathingly. "Well, answer."

"I—I do not know."

"I half-begin to believe in your prudence and modesty," he observed, a doubtful quality in the low voice. Laura was helpless to reply. "You would make a pretty heroine in a story of romance."

Laura's wits began to assemble themselves. "I thank you, my lord. There is no one to play the hero in such a tale."

"No? Lord Greystan covets that role." His tone was casual.

Laura stiffened. "I cannot believe that, sir. It is merely that opposition makes him stubborn. He has gone on to other pursuits. The whole matter has faded from his mind. Besides," she added forthrightly, a dimple appearing, "the gentleman is rather more suited to the role of villain."

Danville said nothing, but a tiny flame lit in his searching gaze as it dwelt on her upturned face and fluctuating color. "Quite a charmer," he stated finally. "Such a face can turn as it will us poor weathervanes of men. Even Mr. Gaunt is smitten. He gives a good account of you. However, Mrs. Meers tells me that your energy flags and that your candle burns late."

"I go on well enough, my lord," said Laura confusedly, unwilling to admit fatigue.

"You are tired-eyed," Danville responded brusquely. "Both Mr. Gaunt and Mrs. Meers will be instructed to lighten your work load."

Laura, overcome that he would trouble himself about her welfare, could only utter a brief "Yes, sir." She saw his hand come out to smooth a tendril behind her ear. His finger followed the line of her cheek and jaw for an instant, and she felt his finger on her mouth. Laura's throat ached, her eyesight dimmed as she gazed up at his smoothly clad shoulders silhouetted against the light. She was filled with a breathtaking awareness; the whole world took on new dimensions.

"You may go now, but return well before dusk."
She did not see his nostrils go thin nor the tightened
muscle in his jaw. She heard his even tones as if
from a great distance and turned blindly away. As
Ned, the groom, handed her up into the gig, she
looked back to see the earl still standing at the head
of the lane, his gloves making a whipping gesture
against his leg.

The gig made the journey to Dolton, and Laura sat
hunched down, staring straight ahead, hearing
nothing. She was unaware of the tears trickling
silently down her face. Her cheeks and lips tingled
where he had touched her. He is beginning to trust
me, she dared to think. A melting sweetness en-
gulfed her. She prayed that she might always live
close to him; she asked for nothing more. But her
whole face turned delicately pink as the thought
intruded of how it would be to touch him, to feel the
formidable line of mouth and chin. His hair would be
thick and soft, like touching satin. The texture of his
skin would be smooth, his breath warm. She shivered in her warm cloak.

As she laid the fire in the stove at her father's
cottage and listened patiently to his rambling village talk, her sound common sense tempered what
she knew to be a flight of fancy. To the earl she was
merely a responsibility placed on him by Lady
Danville. When Caroline Venner became his lady,
she, Laura, would return to this cottage and resume
with some degree of contentment the life that had
originally been intended for her.

Mindful of Lord Danville's instruction not to lin-
ger, she embraced the old man, and carrying a
bundle of his clothing under her arm, she handed it
to Ned before stepping up into the gig. Neither of
them noticed a closed carriage standing in front of

the Sign of the Hart, the inn in Dolton, or that the
driver took up his reins at the same moment the gig
turned into the road. The groom, anxious to get back
to his afternoon tankard of ale, urged the nag on. As
they came out into the country and approached a
winding road through a wood, Ned heard the sound
of wheels and saw the carriage coming closer, its
driver having whipped up the horses. Ned thought
little of it. There was plenty of room for the vehicle
to pass.

It passed with no difficulty and disappeared
around a bend. As they came around the same curve,
Laura saw that the carriage had stopped and barred
the road. The driver made a friendly gesture with
his whip as the gig drew near.

"What's amiss?" called Ned, and the words were
barely out before the carriage door opened and out
stepped a swarthy respectable-looking man dressed
neatly and soberly. The groom stepped down from
the gig, and the man, with a self-possessed air,
reached up to the driver, who handed him a wicked-
looking truncheon. Ned's arm came up too late.
With a thud the truncheon connected, and Ned went
down. Laura cried out and sprang down from the gig
to go to his aid. A strong arm seized her by the waist.
She was unceremoniously tossed into the carriage.

Laura was a strong girl, but her flailing arms and
strugglings were useless. Heedless of her screams,
the man held her wrists and bound them with a soft
cord. "What you need, miss, is a little lockjaw.
Screaming won't help."

"You devil! You've killed Ned! Let me out of here!"

"Easy there, miss. The louder you shriek, the
tighter I'll muzzle you," he said harshly. He drew a
silk kerchief from his pocket, forcing its folds between her teeth and tying it securely in back. She

could only whimper. "There, now, we'll have silence. I'm a quiet man myself."

The carriage lumbered on. Laura saw nothing through the drawn curtains. Resolving to conserve her strength, she sat quietly in her corner. Opposite her, her narrow-faced captor sat with folded arms, sometimes looking at her and sometimes peeking out through a crack in the curtains. She judged that he was some kind of superior servant, obviously of foreign extraction. His chief trait seemed to be his remarkable composure. He looked so steady-nerved and so calm that he made Laura shiver.

At length he addressed her. "My name is Anton, ma'am. You will be seeing me a great deal. The master has given orders concerning you. I may say that he's not one to be disobeyed. You're to be carried to our destination and not a mark on you, he says. The gag may chafe some, but that can't be helped. Orders are that you'll not be harmed. Best rest, miss, there'll be no stopping along the way except to change horses. Never fear but what you'll be made comfortable once we get there. I may say," he added without a smile, "the master has his usual cultivated taste."

With that he closed his lips and leaned back, while Laura moved restlessly. The only person who could have desired to kidnap her was Lord Greystan, and she would never never yield to him. Her feet had not been tied. Perhaps she could escape along the way, even if she hurt herself in the attempt. She would watch for a chance. The man Anton saw her relax, her lids half-closed. All the while she looked from under her lashes, estimating the distance to the door handle, thinking desperately of tumbling out into the road should the carriage slow down.

Mile after mile went by, each mile carrying her

farther away from Glendon. She would never see it
again, she thought desolately. Lord Danville might
easily assume that she had left willingly, that she
had made an assignation with her abductor and had
known that Ned would be attacked. She writhed in
her seat at the thought. She had dared to think that
his severity and mistrust of her had lessened. Only
two days ago he had come upon her as she hummed
and did her mending in the garden.

"Your fingers go skipping at their work, and your
voice goes sweetly with your fingers," he had commented.

She had started up. "I like sewing, my lord."

"It looks tedious."

"But it is easier to think when one's fingers are
occupied," she had rejoined.

"I begin to have a higher opinion of your understanding. In fact," he had added half-cynically, "you
reproach us all with your cottage perfections: beauty, virtue, goodness."

Now he would be sure that she possessed none of
these qualities, Laura reflected drearily. She felt as
though she was at the bottom of a deep well whose
walls gave no foothold for climbing out.

The coach slowed and finally stopped. She heard
voices. They seemed to be in an inn yard. The driver
spoke to an ostler demanding a change of horses.
Anton sat with his all-seeing eyes focused on her.
Laura was thirsty and hungry, but she cared nothing for that. She watched warily from half-closed
lids as Anton leaned toward the left-hand window,
letting it down and pushing the curtain aside. He
swore softly at the driver, ordering him to hurry the
business.

"Damn you, Jarvis, prod those sluggards. We're
behindhand."

As he spoke, Laura made a dive for the handle on the opposite door. The door opened. She had a glimpse of a brick wall opposite. As she tumbled out of the coach, she felt a pull on her skirts. She could not right herself, and her cheek struck the ground. Dazed, she looked up to see Anton standing over her, his composure shaken and his face pale. In a trice he had her under the arms and back in the coach.

"Some cove kickin' up a rumpus." It was a man's voice, and Laura drummed her feet against the floor until Anton silently took both ankles and tied them securely.

"Eh, what's the ruckus in there?" The interested bystander was speaking to the driver.

"Master's takin' a gentleman home. Ye know how it goes. Fellow's been dipping deep, kept on swallowing balls of fire," explained the driver. "These job horses better be able to go their length," he went on to the ostler.

Anton pushed aside the curtain and said, "Best get under way, Jarvis. Dashed if Abbott's not looking queasy. And then," he went on, looking across at Laura, "you'll be in a rare hobble when your wife sees you."

Nothing more was heard from the bystander, and in a few moments the driver got the coach under way. Anton's gaze dwelt on the bruise on Laura's cheek, although if the truth were told, her shoulder pained her even more.

"Now the devil's to pay," he stated grimly. "I told you the master's strict in his notions. What a hurly-burly girl you are. Well, the fellow with the muffler's been gulled, anyway." He shrugged and folded his arms.

After that they traveled in silence. It seemed endless to Laura. Besides her aches and pains, she

was faint from hunger and thirst. She finally fell
into a kind of doze, seeing and hearing everything as
if from a great distance. They clattered over city
streets. There were sounds of many voices and other
vehicles. When the coach finally stopped and Anton
lifted her out, it was night. She was carried into a
house, through a hall, to an upstairs room, where
she was gently laid on a couch. She was loosed from
her bonds; her jaw was swollen from the gag and her
wrists tingled. Laura lifted heavy lids to find Anton
bringing his gaze to bear on her damaged cheek.

"Thanks be the master won't be seeing you for a
day or two; you'll be looking more fit. Now, miss,
there's everything for your comfort in this room. I'll
bespeak a meal for you at once. A hip bath will be
brought up tomorrow. Only thing missing is a lady's
maid. Can you maid yourself?" He attempted a
smile, but it seemed to Laura that the same expression might be seen on the face of a keeper throwing
food to a caged animal.

She tried to speak, the words coming with difficulty around a swollen tongue. "You needn't try to
cozen me. You've sold yourself to the devil."

Anton had the grace to look a little taken aback.
"A proper set-down, ma'am. At least you're not a
female who turns herself into a watering pot or has
the vapors."

Too tired and bewildered to answer him, Laura's
head fell back on the sofa.

"I'll be up in a trice with a good meal, miss. I've
orders you must eat it." He left the room and she
heard a well-oiled lock click into place.

At length Anton returned with a tray. The mouth-
watering odor of a rich soup was tempting.

"You'll feel better after you eat, and I have here a
good salve for your cheek." He folded his arms and

stood at the door, evidently set on overseeing her meal. After she had made a good try at the soup and a slice of York ham with crunchy bread, he silently took the tray and departed, locking the door after him.

In the next two days, Laura explored her elegant one-room prison. It had two windows looking out on brick-walled buildings across an alley. They were windowless and appeared to be warehouses. Her room was luxuriously carpeted and furnished in pale beiges and greens. The bed was comfortable, the sheets silken. Two scenic watercolors hung on the walls. A shelf was filled with a nice choice of books and fashion periodicals that might appeal to a woman. Laura was in no mood for them and wore a path in the green carpet as she paced back and forth.

Anton brought her meals, although there were evidently others belowstairs. She heard their voices. One evening an altercation broke out below, and the voices were raised. It was soon quelled, probably by the severe Anton. Laura herself had made no outcry or escape attempt as yet. She realized the hopelessness of it but waited for an opportunity and measured her chances.

Lord Greystan would be coming soon—of that she was certain. But he would never succeed in his attempt to seduce her. From underneath the bed she had worked loose a stout piece of wood. She kept it under the mattress at night and hidden behind a cushion in the daytime. It would serve to give him a stunning blow over the head. Whether she cracked his skull and swung for it, she did not care. She knew only that she would become no man's light-o'-love. Her mother's and Lady Danville's precepts rang in her ears and she would never forget them. Lord Greystan inspired only hatred and fear in her.

On the fifth day of her captivity she had been served a thick slice of beef for lunch, and a sharp little knife had been on her tray along with a fork and spoon. The knife found its way to a fold in her skirt. As Anton removed the tray, she diverted his attention by announcing that she would that evening begin a hunger strike.

Anton had rasped at her, "That you won't, miss, for I will hand-feed you myself and force the food down your throat. The master won't have it." He stood over her holding the tray and looking for once quite fierce.

"I confess that the thought of your force-feeding me is not an attractive one," she had replied, glad she had upset his composure. He had not answered but had left the room in a hurry, his jaw working. That had been fifteen minutes ago, and she dared to hope that the knife had not been missed.

But her heart came up in her throat as she heard firm footsteps on the stairs.

12
CHAPTER

Nicholas was awakened by his man at an early hour. He generally kept town hours even in the country, retiring late and often sleeping until noon. His powerful frame intimidating even as he lay in bed, he threw back the covers, the steely look from his low-lidded eyes causing that worthy to quake.

"Sorry, sir. I was quite taken aback. Lord Danville's below."

"And you told his lordship that I was abed?"

"Yes, sir. All on a sudden he made for the stairs. I—I thought it best to come up myself, sir."

"Bring trousers and a shirt," instructed Mr. Venner shortly.

Five minutes later Nicholas, clad in fawn-colored trousers and a lawn shirt, came upon the earl in the parlor. Danville, standing at a window, wheeled to face him, his aspect impatient and formidable. Nick's heavy eyebrows rose in surprise.

"What the devil do you mean raising a fellow from bed at this hour?"

"Never mind that," came the sharp retort. "Where's Greystan?"

"Gone back to town these several days," Nick replied. "What's put you on your high ropes?"

"When did he leave?" Danville had not left the window. He stood there motionless, self-contained.

"Why, Tuesday week, I believe it was," Nick answered, rubbing his chin, at a loss to understand his friend.

"Greystan has probably made off with Laura." The tone was harsh.

"Laura? The maidservant? Not likely. I was certain I had scotched that affair. This last visit Greystan's spent time at the inn in Dolton. Allaire and I smoked out a pretty chambermaid for him."

"More likely he was making arrangements to abduct the girl. She was seized last evening just outside Dolton and taken away in a carriage. My groom was found senseless beside the gig."

"Stab me! Could it be?" Nick exclaimed. "Grey's mad-brained. Always knew he was bent on bedding as many females as he could. But when all's said and done, the girl's a honey pot. It could have been some other chap. You never know with females of that stamp."

Danville advanced toward him, menace in his stride. "Stubble it! You'll not cut up the girl's character."

Nicholas retreated a step, his hand raised defensively. "As you say, Evelyn. You needn't come the ugly. Thought you considered the girl beneath your notice."

The earl turned away, a sober look settling on his countenance. "I have insensibly been brought to admire her, observing as I have her gracefulness, humility, and innocence. But enough of that. Are you sure that Greystan set out for London?"

"That was his destination."

At that moment the dainty form of Caroline Venner appeared in the opening. She looked fetching in a thin morning gown of hyacinth blue, a lacy apron around her waist suggesting that she had been engaged in womanly chores.

"Evelyn!" she exclaimed, her hands coming up in surprise. "And Nick already up?" She looked at her brother.

"Danville's uncovered a hornet's nest concerning Grey," Nick explained.

The earl bowed, noting the lady's look of morning perfection.

"Grey?" she asked in charming confusion. "But he's in London."

"Greystan took a fancy to Laura. You remember her?" Nick winked slyly at her.

"Oh, yes, the servant who gave Harris so much trouble," she answered primly. She did not see the inquiring lift of the earl's brow at this remark.

As Nick gave his sister the particulars of the story, Caroline's mouth opened in disbelief. Before she could comment, however, the earl cut in. "Exactly what was Harris' difficulty with Laura?"

"Why, it was during Lady Danville's illness, Laura was so insistent on taking over Harris' duties."

"I believe my mother was always happy to have Laura as a companion but forbade her to come to the sickroom lest she catch the infection."

"You are quite right. But even Father had to reprove Laura for her encroaching ways."

"Strange. The girl has made every effort to please at Glendon. Since she was not permitted the sickroom, how was she occupied during that time?"

"I believe the housekeeper gave her other duties. There was much to do what with the dear lady's illness and Nick and his friends here." Caroline looked grave and demure as she fingered her dark curls.

"Duties which brought her under Greystan's notice perhaps?" he asked cynically. This was getting
close to home, and Caroline fidgeted as she looked at
her brother.

"Really, Evelyn, I cannot say. What goes on belowstairs can be no concern of mine."

"My mother held that such matters are never too
trifling for the notice of a good mistress." He looked
at her with an oddly persistent gaze.

Nick, seeing his sister's uneasiness, came to her
rescue. "However, it came about, Greystan did develop a *tendre* for the girl, but it's my belief it was
only temporary."

"I shall soon find out," replied Danville, his lips
thinning.

"And what will you do when you corner him?"
inquired Nick.

"Cut his liver out and fry it." With that his
lordship bowed briefly and strode from the room.

"By God if I ever saw such an inferno," Nick
remarked. "I wouldn't hazard a groat on Grey's life
if Danville finds him."

But Caroline could summon no concern over Lord
Greystan's fate. Taken up with the thought that the
earl's image of her might have been damaged, she
worried lest Danville discover that she had had a
part in Laura's disappearance.

"I don't care a rap about Grey."

"You did at one time. You're a heartless piece,
Caro," he remarked, scanning her face. "Wouldn't be
surprised if Danville wasn't having second thoughts
today. Excessively awkward if he begins to look
beneath that pretty shell of a face."

"Says the kettle to the pot," she snapped. "You've
frequented every den of iniquity from Venice to
London."

"But all my fevers have taught me a certain discretion," replied her brother.

"Do you not think that Evelyn shows an extraordinary concern for Laura?"

"Danville won't stand still for interference in his affairs. After all, she was a valuable servant to his mother."

Caroline looked at her brother uncertainly and asked in a subdued tone, "You don't think Evelyn is losing his regard for me?"

"I daresay he'll come around all right and tight after this bustle is over." Nick shrugged carelessly.

On Danville's return to Glendon he informed Yeats that he would leave for London but first would see Mrs. Meers in his study. The housekeeper answered the summons, the usual cheerfulness gone from her face and her eyes red from weeping.

"Beccles is packing your things, my lord. Excuse me, sir, but I do be hoping your lordship is of a mind to ferret out what's happened to Laura."

"Take comfort, Mrs. Meers. That is my intention in going to London. But first answer me a few questions. You spoke once of Harris' dislike of Laura. You may speak freely to me about the whole matter. I have a regard for your good sense."

Mrs. Meers hesitated. "I'm not one to pick a hole in anyone's coat, sir, and Harris loved the mistress. But she couldn't abide that my lady loved Laura more."

"Understandable. How far did she carry her grudge?"

"I don't know the whole of it, my lord. Harris gave Laura what-for here at Glendon, but when Lady Danville was ill at the Venner residence, it's my belief matters got out of hand."

"Go on, Mrs. Meers," urged the earl, for Mrs. Meers had folded her hands and stood obstinately silent.

"It's not for me to speak daggers against my betters, sir."

"I assume you refer to one of the Venner family. Who? Sir Richard?"

"Harris did talk of Sir Richard giving Laura a set-down," Mrs. Meers muttered unwillingly. "And he wasn't the only one, I'll warrant, but Laura kept her tongue between her teeth."

"And now we come to your real thoughts, Mrs. Meers, which I daresay are near the truth. I am persuaded that for Laura's sake you will speak out."

"Well, my lord, it's my belief Miss Venner has Harris in her pocket." Mrs. Meers pressed her lips together.

"If you are correct, I wonder why." Danville looked thoughtful. He took a sudden decision. "Say nothing of this to Harris and send her to me."

Mrs. Meers could not hide a look of satisfaction at this order.

When Harris appeared before his desk, the earl regarded her so intently and for so long that her thin fingers began to twitch with apprehension.

"I believe you were genuinely fond of your mistress, Harris. How is it, then, that you have so quickly forgotten her and given your devotion to Miss Caroline Venner?" Fright and grief showed in Harris' face; she looked dazedly at him, unable to answer. "Have you been tempted into actions that would have distressed my mother?"

"It's— I was under Miss Venner's orders when my lady lay ill in her house, my lord."

Sternly reminding Harris that she owed no allegiance to Miss Venner, he continued to question the

maid, persistently wearing down her resistance
until the floodgates opened and she began to babble,
almost incoherently. When Harris revealed that
Caroline Venner had schemed to bring Laura to
Greystan's notice, a look of complete shock crossed
his face, followed by an expression of such cold
contempt that Harris quailed and retreated from the
desk. Resolving that Harris must not contact Caroline again, Danville quieted the maid. Knowing that
she had a brother who ran a smithy in Devon, he
arranged that she visit him there forthwith. He
would resolve her case when he had time. As it was,
he had postponed his departure for London too long.

The earl rode into London late in the afternoon
and made straight for Lord Greystan's house in
Brook Street. He found the residence in darkness,
but his loud knocking finally brought a gloomy and
impassive butler to the door. Reluctantly stepping
back, he bowed and allowed Lord Danville to step in.

"Lord Greystan is not at home, sir. He left town a
week ago."

This piece of information brought a snarl from
Danville, and he took the dignified man by the
throat, pushing him against the paneled wall. Pressure against his windpipe brought the blood into the
unfortunate man's face.

"More definite information, please," Danville ordered, easing the pressure.

"Begging your pardon," wheezed the butler, his
eyes goggling, "the master left suddenlike and put
me in charge of the house while he's away."

"And that is all you know?"

"All, sir, I promise you."

Disgusted, Danville stalked out, and after a
change of clothing at his own town house, he made
for Boodle's, that elegant rendezvous of idle and

gambling gentlemen. Here, with studied indifference, he questioned Mr. Converse and Viscount Blanton, two of Greystan's familiars.

"Fellow's taken off mighty sudden, left town without crying off from an engagement he had with me at Tattersall's. Rumor is there was a bit of unpleasantness with Lasley," Mr. Converse reported.

"All hush-hush, what I'm saying," confided the viscount. "All I know is Lasley's gone off, too. Wouldn't surprise me if the two of them hadn't come to cuffs. Greystan's been touchy ever since he came back from the country."

"Some sort of a flame-up," Mr. Converse agreed knowingly. "If you ask me, they'll neither one show their faces for a while."

Seeing that he could extract nothing more from the two, the earl took himself off in search of Mr. Allaire. He finally cornered that gentleman in a gaming house run by a Mrs. Villiers in Conduit Street. Allaire, always a spectator of the fads and whims of a fast rackety set, was alone at a table in the corner, having dipped deep from a bottle of brandy. He raised a brow and motioned carelessly for Danville to join him.

"Thought you firmly anchored in the country."

"I was. Where's Greystan?"

"Not in town."

"I know that, and I don't mean to be put off. You know of his pursuit of my mother's maidservant, Laura. He seems to have made off with her. I'll have his hide for it."

Allaire took a while to digest this information, then began to shake his head in amiable disagreement. "Not possible," he said positively.

"Why?"

"Not to be noised about, but Grey's gone abroad. France, I believe. Left a week ago."

"You're sure?"

"Of course I am." Mr. Allaire looked injured. "Had a dispute with Lasley at Lasley's house. I was there. Called Lasley out."

"You mean a duel?"

"Exactly. Whole affair was disgraceful. Lasley called Grey's coat an affront to the eye. Grey challenged him. Grey called on me to second him. Can't think why I consented to such an outrageous thing; we were all foxed, of course."

"Well, I'll be damned."

"You may well say so. Not proud of my part in it. Jacobs was there. The four of us made a night of it at Lasley's anyway, then set off for Hyde Park in a pair of hackney carriages like a pretty set of gudgeons." A slow smile dawned in Mr. Allaire's befuddled expression. The events of that evening were returning. "Dampish night."

Seeing that Allaire was a trifle bosky and not to be hurried, Danville sat down and poured himself a brandy. "Yes? What happened?"

"Amusing thing. Just as we turned into the park, we saw an empty hearse. Grey pokes his head out of the window and says, 'Hey, you with the hell-cart, if you'll wait I'll give you a fare.'"

The earl smiled, but only just barely. "That's neither here nor there. Then what?"

"We came to a paved triangle behind a church. Lasley stripped off his coat, but Grey only closed his. They took their places, saluted, and crossed swords. I could see at once that Lasley was no swordsman. He made a few clumsy rushes, parrying wildly. Grey played with him awhile, but only meant to pink him.

Then Grey slipped and was down, his elbow striking the pavement. Lasley held off. Grey's arm was numb. He thrust strongly over Lasley's guard and ran him through the chest."

"How is Lasley?"

"Off in the country. It was a high chest thrust, he'll recover. Grey took off for the Continent the same day."

"How you came to mingle with such a set of fools is past understanding. You then declare that Grey could have had nothing to do with the abduction of Laura?"

"How could he? Impossible. Went off in such a dashed hurry."

"The devil's in it now," snapped Danville, rising from his chair. "I'll call around in the morning when your head is clearer. Don't try to stand while the room is in motion."

Allaire gave him a confused look as he picked up his goblet.

But Allaire's clear head the next morning held very little more information than he had already given, and Lord Danville was at a standstill in his quest for Laura's whereabouts. After two more days in London, he returned to Glendon, thinking that a clue there had possibly been overlooked. He was determined to find the girl.

On the third afternoon he rode to the Venner residence, a look of distaste on his face as the door was opened to him by Caroline. He bowed over her hand, viewing with careless disregard the perfection of her mauve crepe gown and the matching ribbons in her dark ringlets. She sensed at once his new indifference.

"Come into the parlor, Evelyn," she invited, and when he stood facing her there, his dark head thrown back in a gesture of disapproval, she went on unsteadily. "You—you look angry."

"I look at you more in sorrow than in anger," he stated. "You cannot be so surprised. Mrs. Meers tells me that you called after I left and asked for Harris. Fortunately or unfortunately, however you look at it, she has been sent away for a time." Caroline looked away, biting at her lower lip. "Did you perhaps want another report from your watcher there?"

A flush colored her cheeks. "I declare I do not know what you mean. I became fond of Harris when she was here with Lady Danville."

Danville said tiredly, "The fat's in the fire, the kettle has boiled over. Harris has confessed her dealings with you and revealed your treatment of Laura. You've run aground, Caroline."

At this crumbling of all her hopes, Caroline closed her eyes. Her ambition to be the next Countess of Danville had failed. She had worked so hard to achieve her end. She had had her eye on the earl for so long, attracted not only by his wealth and position but also by the man himself. Now she, who usually could twist facts to suit her fancy, was without a defense. Her cunning ingenuity temporarily deserted her.

"I—I can only say that I did what I did because of my fondness for you."

"A unique way of showing fondness, setting up a spy in my home and plotting the seduction of a maidservant."

"You—you won't overlook it?"

"How is it possible?" he asked impatiently. "I had thought you above reproach; your conduct has been unprincipled, to say the least. But we won't discuss it. Greystan left the country before Laura was abducted. If you know anything that I do not about her disappearance, I charge you to tell me." He took her by the chin and raised her face to look into it searchingly.

"No—no, I do not. I thought Grey had abducted her."

"Where's Nick?"

"He went back to town."

He saw the tears finally appear and slide down her cheeks. A muscle tautened in his jaw, and he withdrew his hand. "Everyone's in town. You'd enjoy the bustle there," he advised quietly. "Perhaps we'll run across each other there."

Caroline looked up to see that he had gone, leaving her drained and empty.

13
CHAPTER

Had the knife been missed? As she heard the determined footsteps on the stairs, Laura was sure of it. She heard another set of footsteps and then Anton's voice.

"If you'll allow me to speak, sir, I should tell you—"

"Not now," came an oddly familiar voice, low and authoritative, that she could not quite recognize.

"It's about the young miss, sir—"

"I said later. Get below." The tone was quiet, but it held menace. Laura heard Anton's retreating footsteps and the turning of the key in the lock. The door opened. She stared, her jaw dropping in disbelief.

Nicholas Venner closed the door and stood regarding her. The gray eyes took their time in making a detailed inspection of her, like someone checking to make sure that nothing was missing. He looked inhuman, untouchable. The bones in his hard face were rigid, his lips were clamped together. She thought she had never seen a face so coldly implacable. A raw fury erupted in his gaze when his eyes rested on her bruised cheek.

"How came you by that black-and-blue cheek?" he asked softly. "I'll have the hide off Anton for this."

"It was not his fault," she returned, white-faced. "I tried to escape and fell from the carriage."

135

"Are you otherwise hurt? I shall soon see." He moved closer.

"No," she answered unsteadily, forcing herself to remain where she was. "Why have you done this?"

"Come now, you are not such an innocent as that. Has no one ever told you that you practice sorcery? You cast a spell on me from the first with that enchanting face and that delicious shape unfairly concealed by bulky servant's garb. Silk and jewels should become you. We shall soon see."

Laura repressed a shudder. Here was a man who frightened her a great deal more than Lord Greystan. She felt that she might have had a chance of escape with Greystan. Nicholas Venner was a man of more dangerous acumen, more discerning, more decisive. She felt as if she were now between the hammer and the anvil. Indignation welled up in her against the injustice of circumstance.

"You'll give me nothing, sir. You are foolish if you think that your foul proceedings will not finally become known."

Nicholas smiled cynically. "Not a chance. Lord Greystan's the prime suspect. After the hubbub is over, it won't matter. As for the pretties I intend for you, I'll lay odds that within a week you'll welcome them."

"How is it that wealth and power can so plot together against lack of experience and low estate? I have done nothing to harm you, yet you would violate every feeling I have about what is right."

His gray eyes faltered for an instant. "It is true that I have taken you against your will, but I hope to change your low opinion of me. To be quite frank, other members of the fair sex have looked upon me with some favor, but I have never doted on any as I do you."

Laura replied with a curl of the lip. "I am sure that you have been badly smitten hundreds of times, and have survived. You hardly know me. This, too, will pass away."

"Mayhap," he said slowly. "But now we shall have the opportunity to become acquainted. The more I see of you, the more enamored I become."

"Can I not appeal to your better instincts? I beg of you to let me go, and—"

Before she could finish, his arm reached for her, tightening around her as she tried to draw away. She was pressed against his tall frame. Her tremors of fear could not be hidden as she felt herself locked in his powerful right arm, her softness crushed to his hardness from chest to knee. For an instant his fingers explored the warm hollow behind her ear. She pushed hard against his chest as revulsion curled through her stomach.

"For shame! You are mad!" As she shivered in his grasp, she felt his hold ease. He fell back.

"Your pardon. I go too fast for you, but the temptation is great. I do not mean to force you or to frighten you, only to show you the pleasures we may share together."

"I wish I may die before I yield to your wicked desires. You forfeit your honor when you take freedoms with me, who am defenseless and in your power."

"Why, here's a pretty sermon, you need a gown and cassock." He was smiling.

"Does it become your station to take a servant girl by force?"

Nicholas became irritated. "Strange girl. I offer you escape from your servitude and intend to surround you with every luxury."

"All stratagems to gain your own ends," she flared. "I want none of it."

"Let be. So far I have robbed you of nothing."

"Except my good name."

"How now? A maidservant's honor?" His mouth thinned in derision. "You are full of pride and perverseness. Is it not natural for a gentleman to love a pretty woman?"

"Only if both be willing." Exhaustion was beginning to show on her pallid face.

"Say no more, little witch, for I will have you." His large hand closed on her arm with bruising force and then eased. "I had thought you easy prey, but I now see that I shall have to course the hare. You are tired. Rest now." His eyes dwelt on her bruised cheek, and he said softly, "I hope to see you soon restored to perfection." He took her hand, and she felt a light kiss on its palm.

When he had gone, her weakened knees gave out, and she sank into the nearest chair. Nicholas Venner's purpose was clear. Experienced man of the world as he was, confident and skillful, he expected her to submit to him finally—even to submit gracefully. To others he was handsome and attractive, but not to her. His touch set her teeth on edge. Only one man had a magnetic pull for her. Laura closed her eyes, and out of the darkness against her lids, his beautiful familiar figure walked toward her. Tall and lean, the figure approached, the expression in the dark eyes inaccessible to her, forever out of reach.

The sound of a voice raised in pleading erupted from below. It sounded like Anton. Laura opened her eyes. Then she heard solid footsteps on the stairs. Nicholas Venner reentered the room and leaned back against the closed door.

"The knife, Laura," he said, a slow smile on his sensual lips. "You are a bad, stupid child."

Laura sat quite still until she saw his long back beginning to straighten away from the door. Hopelessly she reached under the cushion and brought out the knife. He leaned over to take it, his hard finger brushing her cheek. "You shan't escape, you know, but before long you will not wish to. Only then will you have any freedom."

He left her then, but she still felt his presence like a dark cloud. How could she ever escape? Laura crept to the window and tried to open it. But even if she could force it up, there was a long drop to the ground. Far to her left was a rooftop, a part of the lower story of the house. If she could get to that rooftop, it might be possible to make another jump to the ground. Or someone might pass below in the alleyway and she could break the window to draw attention to her predicament. What remote possibilities these were. She went back to the bed and lay down. Worn out, she drifted into sleep, and when she awoke, it was nighttime. Candlelight made the room inviting and a fire had been lit. The austere Anton was placing a well-filled tray on a table.

"You have had a good rest, miss. Master Nicholas has left word that he will return in the morning." Laura sat up, still not quite awake. "Meanwhile, miss, when you have eaten, I'll bring a tub for your bath. Mr. Venner regrets that you will have to wait for a change of clothing. Madame Brissarde has been given your measurements, and the garments will begin arriving tomorrow."

"At any rate you are a capable tool of your master, Anton," she said bitterly.

Impervious to this remark, the servant replied, "I strive to please, miss. Mr. Venner regrets that he

cannot supply you with the services of a maid."
When Laura made no answer, he went on, "I will
return for the tray, ma'am."

Laura was hungry, and the covered dishes held
tempting delicacies—turtle soup, roast duckling, a
syllabub of fruit. When Anton returned for the tray,
he looked approvingly at its emptiness. Soon he was
back with a tub, and he made several trips for hot
water. Laura positioned a chair under the door
handle and stayed in the hot water until it cooled;
the warmth eased the pain in her bruised shoulder. I
cannot afford to be ill or weak, she thought. I must
be able to act at once if an opportunity comes to get
away.

After a restless night she awoke to a rapping at
the door. The night before she had refused to admit
Anton when he returned for the tub, and she had left
the chair under the door. Quickly she left the bed.
She was fully dressed in the clothing she had worn
before.

"Open up, Laura, or I'll have the door down." It
was Nicholas Venner's angry voice.

Plucking up her courage, Laura went to admit
him, and when he stood glowering at her, she said
boldly, "I can see you are in high force today, sir."

His brows shot up in surprise at this forwardness.
"Little vixen! Anton should have sent word that you
had blocked the door."

"I am entitled to some privacy." His gray eyes
focused on her, and she wished she had not spoken,
because their expression was ominous.

"Anton or I must have access to the room at all
times. Disobey me in this, and you will wish you had
not." She saw the hardening of the already hard
mouth.

Laura shrugged. "As you will," she said resigned-ly. There was little use in arguing with him. She must save her energy for later, when the time came to resist his advances.

Nicholas stood contemplating her for a long mo-ment. Satisfied that she would comply with his command, he opened the door and called to Anton, who awaited his pleasure below. "You may bring the boxes. Later you may arrange everything in the wardrobe. You must allow Anton to perform some of the duties of a lady's maid, ma'am, and make allowance for his inexperience." Anton came into the room with a number of boxes that he laid on the bed. Nicholas waved him from the room and strolled to the bed.

"Come and see the pretties. Surely you are not immune to pretty gowns and fripperies?" Out of the boxes came a sea of ruffles and flounces—lovely gowns of all types, each one beautifully made. Nich-olas uncovered a box of petticoats and night clothes in palest yellows and pinks. Another box held slip-pers, another silk hose and underthings.

Laura looked at everything with shame. How could he put her to the blush like this? He must have performed these same acts many times before. She supposed that there would always be some new damsel ready to fall like ripe fruit into his hand. Life had never denied him anything. He knew he had only to stretch out a hand to get what he wanted. He was impervious. But she, too, was impervious in her own way. Her mind and heart yearned only for the approval and esteem of another more demanding and difficult gentleman. Whether or not she ever saw him again, the course of her feelings would not change.

"I have never hoped to possess such finery, and you are foolish if you think to entice me with it," she said bluntly.

He turned, an edge in the steel-gray eyes. "You have no choice, ma'am. Shall I maid you?" He drew out a morning dress of sprigged muslin. "This should be appropriate. I have a mind to see how you look in presentable apparel."

"Surely you would do nothing by force."

"I would as lief do it as not in this case." He smiled knowingly at her. "Ungrateful baggage. I shall leave you for a short time and allow you to make up your mind." With a lazy bow, he made for the door.

It did not take Laura long to come to a decision. Hastily she removed all her old clothes and put on the new, her fingers clumsily fastening the tiny buttons. In her hurry, the heavy coil of her hair had come loose, and when Nicholas reentered the room, he paused in astonishment at the beauty unveiled before him. The close fit of the dress revealed the lines of her developing figure, tiny of waist and suggesting the long line from hip to knee. A blush suffused her lovely face, half turned from him. She felt exposed in these unfamiliar garments, so different from her enveloping black uniform. Her hand came up in embarrassment to twine through a lock of bright hair that lay on her neck. Her head was down, trying not to see his dark hawklike face.

"No need for the curling tongs," he said huskily, his eyes on her hair. Laura could not speak. The natural waves swept back from her white brow, and delicate tendrils of curls sprang back from her temples and swirled around her ears. "It is outrageous hair, such as would put the most disgraceful thoughts into a man's head." Nicholas advanced toward her, taking her hand and pulling her inflexibly toward him. One of his hands came up to bury itself in her hair. Then she felt his right arm tightening around her. The sensation of fright hurt her throat. Her head was pulled back and his eyes searched her face.

"I like your hair loose," he muttered. His lips closed over her own in a long and savage kiss. It went on and on. Laura felt as if she were smothering and might faint. When he lifted his head, he saw the waxen color of her face; she would have fallen if he had not been supporting her. "I do not mean to frighten you, but I was carried away," he whispered.

Laura felt herself supported to a chair and deposited gently. In a moment he was beside her with a glass of brandy. He held it to her lips, and she felt the warmth flow through her when she sipped from the glass.

"How little you know," he said then. "How innocent you are. I hope to persuade you to encourage my advances. The pleasures of the flesh are not limited to men only, you know."

"I would rather be set loose in the middle of the wildest moor in England than to be here with you," she said, and suddenly overcome, she buried her face in her hands and sobbed bitterly.

Nicholas stood above her for some time, letting her cry. His face had taken on a gravity that it did not often wear. When she had quieted so that he heard only occasional hiccups and sniffles, he observed wryly, "I believe this is the first time that a kiss of mine has cast a female into such a gloom." As he spoke, his fingers began to caress the back of her neck.

She shrank away, raising her tear-filled eyes to his. "Can you not let me be? Has no woman ever been indifferent to you?"

"None that I ever wanted," he said softly.

"Excepting me," she replied stubbornly.

He smiled. Then he sat down in an opposite chair, stretching out his legs and pushing his hands deep into his pockets. "I shall have you, you know. Most women become damned tiring, but not you. When I am away from you, I see you plainly in my mind's eye, all your pretty poses and changes of expression. I believe I even know how you will look as an old lady."

Laura grew red as fire and looked away, disconcerted by his plain speaking. No one had ever talked to her in this manner. When she glanced back, the steel-gray eyes glinted with laughter. As he sat there, he was devastatingly attractive. He could not know how immune she was to his attraction. A twist of pain caught her under the ribs; her heart had already been tamed by another hand.

"You must learn not to put on those dismal grave looks," chided Nicholas softly. "We must take time to become properly acquainted. I shall remember that I am a gentleman. My intention is not to compel but to persuade. I have complete faith in my powers of persuasion, and finally your willing consent." Laura thought she saw complacency and confidence in his expression. He would find that soft words and ruses availed him nothing. She was immune to the blackest magic he could devise. But she feared him, for she was certain his forbearance would not last forever.

"Usually the female casts out lures to me. Now the process is to be reversed," he promised, a sardonic twist to his mouth.

In the days that followed, Laura saw that Nicholas Venner had mapped a campaign and would persist in it. Under his critical gaze, she learned to wear with grace the elegant gowns he had ordered for her, knowing that protest was useless. Often he took his meals with her, the table set with the finest linen and china. Impatient when she was silent, he forced her to converse. It was as if he meant to test her faculties and discover her thoughts. His treatment of her had none of the fine gentleman-servant relationship; there was nothing stiff or condescending in his manner. It was the first time that Laura had had contact as an equal with a sophisticated, well-informed mind. A rake he might be, but he was as needle-witted as they come.

When the conversation was finished, he might set her on his knee and stroke her cheeks and neck or kiss her lightly, an odd gleam far back in his eyes. She would glare mutely at him, but knowing that he held himself in check, she submitted. She knew the consequences if she should put up a struggle.

Nicholas gave her a map of London and pointed out the places of interest, all of which was new and fascinating learning. He described the many places he had visited and opened for Laura the world of travel. When he spoke with intimate knowledge of Venice, she did not know that his stay at Lady Pauling's Palazzo Rivaldi had been other than that of a friend-to-friend.

"No collection of paintings is more overwhelming than the huge series of Tintorettos in the Scuola di San Rocco. Many of them cannot be understood. I have seen men moved to tears as they stand before the immense masterpiece of the *Crucifixion*."

"And the Basilica? What is it like?"

"Stupendous, but what I recall most vividly are the pigeons who enter slyly and march pompously up the nave. One cannot escape the animal world in Venice. Thousands of crabs scuttle along the waterlines. Mice often scurried before me down the corridors of the palace. And thousands of cats peer from the pedestals and sit in the gardens." He watched with interest her rapt expression and proceeded to tell her of the food and the abundance of fruits and vegetables.

"The *calamari* soup is made of squid cooked in their own ink—not to my taste. Massive mushrooms are cooked like steak. I like their sweet-sour muskmelons—sour in the stomach if not soberly eaten."

"I wonder that you ate them, then," she said daringly.

"Minx," he said, laughing and reaching out to tweak her cheek.

Laura longed to ask if her absence had affected Lord Danville, but somehow his name could not pass her lips. Surely, if only for the sake of his pride, he would have ordered an inquiry into the disappearance of a servant that his mother had valued. On an evening when Nicholas had plied her with two glasses of Madeira, she finally plucked up her courage.

"Did—did Lord Danville ever seek to find out what happened to me?" She stood at the window so that he could not read her face.

"Naturally," returned Nicholas. "I wonder that you had not asked before. Danville doesn't take kindly to meddling in his affairs. He assumed, as did you and everyone, that Lord Greystan had abducted you."

"Then, what?"

"Danville confronted Caroline and me. I confess to throwing a red herring in his path. He went off to London in pursuit of Greystan."

Laura heard these words with a rush of joy.

Whatever his reasons, he had made a push to find her. He might not have given up. Even now, he might still be seeking her.

"However, events saved my conscience somewhat. Greystan's in the clear, went off to the Continent before you disappeared. What happened to you remains a mystery, a mystery that I shall do nothing to clarify," he added cynically. To her disappointment, he then went on to change the subject. But that night and many nights she lay awake, a hundred questions on her mind. Did Lord Danville assume that she had gone willingly? Had he shown any emotion at all at her disappearance? Probably he had resumed the even tenor of his days—hunting, escorting Caroline Venner, journeying to London when the fancy took him. Meanwhile, she was caught in a trap she could not escape.

One evening Nicholas brought her a flat leather box, presenting it with a ceremonious bow. She wore a gold silk gown, its high waist accented with a wide band of darker gold.

"Indulge me by accepting a gift," he begged. As she hesitated, he went on, "I expect you to exclaim with delight, as so many ladies of my acquaintance would. Open it."

Laura lifted the lid. Inside was a rope of lustrous pearls. "They are beautiful, but you know my feelings. I cannot in conscience accept them."

"I debated between diamonds and pearls," he said gravely, as if she had not spoken, "but pearls better become your young innocence."

"I cannot," she persisted.

"Ungrateful baggage," he said, unmoved. "It is true that no man gives jewels to a pretty woman without some designs on her. But I thought perhaps you would be tempted by their beauty."

Laura turned aside and shook her head. He took them from the box and fastened them, seeing as he did so her shudder as the necklace fell into place around her neck. "Whether you like it or not, you must wear them to gratify me. Silk and jewels become you." He looked at her for a while then, seeing how well the pearls set off the elegant simplicity of the gown and also how she hung her head as if ashamed. When he left her, it was a relief to take them off and return them to the box.

Nicholas was absent the next day, but late the day following, he appeared in buckskins and top boots, looking rather pale and declaring that his head felt like a balloon. He had Anton bring him a glass of a grayish substance that he called a clincher, and after swallowing this life-giving fluid, his appearance and temper improved.

"Ran aground at Blake's hunting seat," he explained apologetically. "Tossed off a glass too many." At Laura's raised brows, he went on. "Blake's getting married and was blue-deviled. Several of us gave him a send-off. Very tolerable port. Assure you, though, that I don't make a habit of dipping deep." Nicholas appeared to be more talkative than usual.

"Well, I am sure it is your own affair, after all," Laura said equably.

"Unexceptionable girl," approved Nick. "Not one of those complaining women. Dash it all, devil of a dust kicked up there. Almost came to blows, some of 'em."

"How, pray?" she asked, interested and, besides, always feeling safer to keep him talking.

"Chap there, Wentworth, had received a wetting in an afternoon rainstorm. Kept complaining he was cold. Danville was there. Probably to silence him, he

plied him with Cognac and warm beer. Didn't shut
Wentworth up, though."

"Then what?" asked Laura, attempting to hide her
quickened interest.

"Lord Bronday was there; he has a caustic wit,
that fellow. Wentworth applied to him for a remedy.
Bronday had had enough. 'Why, what the devil, fire
a pistol down your throat,' he barked."

Nicholas looked fascinated as Laura laughed
aloud, the first time he had heard her. "How did it
end?" she asked.

"Wentworth took offense, grabbed Bronday by his
neckcloth. Danville separated them, then took his
leave."

"Was Lord Danville angry?"

"Bored, more like. But then he always looks that
way of late."

Laura was silent, wondering why the earl appeared bored, and Nicholas went on to say, "I shall
be riding to Dolton for a day or two. Anton will be
responsible for all going well here." He looked
suddenly concerned. "It goes against the pluck with
me to keep you so confined, but there's no other
way."

"True, sir, no way, unless you give up your dishon-
orable resolve to keep me here." She gave him a
direct look, and the thought crossed her mind that
he appeared momentarily conscience-stricken. But
it could not be. Nicholas would never think it
necessary to justify his actions.

"Enough of your long face," he said irritably.
"What favor may I do for you before I go?"

"Nothing, sir. But I am troubled about my father.
He lives in a cottage in Dolton. Would—could you
find out how he is progressing?"

"I believe I may do so without arousing suspicion," he agreed. She could not know that Nicholas had no real desire to visit his family. His inclination was always to stay at the small house where he held her prisoner. He grudged the time spent at the gaming tables or attending routs or balls. It was all a careful stratagem to throw dust in the eyes of anyone, especially Lord Danville, who might look into Nick Venner's movements.

"When I questioned you before, you told me that you were a foundling. Has an inquiry ever come from your real parents?" he asked curiously.

"Never, and it will not happen now. I could not have had dearer real parents than my foster parents have been, poor and lowly though they were."

"As you say. By now I am well aware that you regard rank and a well-lined purse as corrupting influences," he observed wryly.

"You mistake me entirely. Only in *your* case," she replied with a saucy smile.

"You take uncommon liberties with my character. It is true that I have had some tough skirmishes with chaperones and mamas. But you're quite beside the bridge if you believe that I value nothing but a reputation as an idler and a heartbreaker." He looked at her with cold gravity.

"I do not think you beyond redemption," Laura answered.

14
CHAPTER

During the time that Nicholas was away, the days passed even more slowly. There was nothing to do but read. Her appetite was poor. Laura missed the out-of-doors, and the healthy glow of color disappeared from her cheeks. Sometimes she dreamed that she was back in the familiar solitude of the home wood at Glendon, running through the trees to the pond where she had first seen the earl. Or she might be taking long trancelike walks in the stormy autumn weather, the wet hair clinging to her face. When her sleep brought her memories of the old church in which she had been christened and confirmed, she would wake with a warm feeling of comfort. But when the proud features and imposing form of Lord Danville appeared in her dreams, she cried out in her sleep and awoke to feel her hands clenched into fists.

Anton was the only person she saw. He performed all the tasks usually done by a maidservant. Nicholas had been gone two days when she noticed that Anton was ailing. His dark complexion was flushed with fever, and he could not smother a dry cough. Laura strongly recommended him to take to his bed, but he would have none of it, asserting gloomily that he had had his orders.

"Of all the nonsensical notions," she said tartly,

incensed at his stubbornness. "Your master values
your services too much to wish you to go into a
decline."

"That's as may be, miss," he answered, "but
there's no trusted person to take my place."

Seeing that she could not reason with him, Laura
gave it up, but the next day his affliction also
became hers. Too squeamish to eat, she rearranged
the food on her plate. Anton was too ill to notice. All
day she lay on the bed, and that night she tossed
with fever. The next day she managed to dress and
staggered to a chair. She sat there in a stupor,
endeavoring to put on a decent appearance whenever the manservant attended her. He commented
huskily on her lack of appetite, and she murmured
that she had eaten something that disagreed with
her. Anton only shook his head and exited with the
tray.

Late that afternoon the door opened. She heard it
but was too tired to open her eyes. "What the devil,"
came Nicholas' voice overloud in her ears. "Why are
you sitting in darkness? Anton!" he bellowed down
the stairs.

"Needn't shout the rafters down. Too loud. Going
for a walk," she mumbled incoherently, and stumbled to her feet. His right arm caught her to him, his
rain-wet cheek refreshing against her hot one.
"Walk in the rain," she whispered.

"My God, you are ill. I should never have left," he
groaned, lifting her and carrying her to the bed.

"Anton ill. Must go to bed," she said, turning her
head into the pillow. He swore softly between his
teeth as he made for the door.

The next thing Laura saw was an aged, kindly
face bending over her. She tried to sit up to ease her
tight breathing. "Lie still. Constriction in the chest

and high fever." He was speaking to someone else, and she saw Nicholas standing at the foot of the bed, his lazy self-confidence gone, the bones in the hard face rigid and his mouth clamped together.

"She should have poultices on her chest, and she should drink as much liquid as possible. Apply cloths to lessen the fever. You have someone to nurse her?" He was evidently a doctor, and he was insistent.

"Naturally," returned Nicholas tightly.

"A neglected cold, I believe, and it is to be hoped that it does not develop into anything more serious. We shall know by morning. These drops I leave are to be taken now and twice during the night."

"Yes, well, never mind that," directed Laura hazily. "Time to go home." Her lids fell. A heavy weight seemed to lie on her chest, and the sound of their voices faded away.

But she was not to be left to rest. A hard arm brought her up from the pillows, and a glass was held to her lips. "Drink," instructed Nicholas sternly, and she was obliged to swallow the bitter stuff in it. He stripped the bed and remade it, rolling her from side to side in the process.

"Let be," she protested, but Nicholas ignored her. Whatever he had given her was making her more drowsy. She felt her clothes removed, and the welcome coolness of compresses applied all over her. Then a poultice soothed her chest. Finally she began to shiver and was soon enveloped in warm blankets. When the fever returned, the same process began again; toward morning she slept soundly.

The next day she was better, and the doctor's visit brought the good news that she should be up and about in a few days. Nicholas made no effort to hide his relief, the set bleakness of his face revealing that

he had noted every change in Laura's breathing
through the night.

"My orders have been well seen to," said the
doctor with a speculative look at Nicholas, thinking
to himself that here was a gentleman who wanted
neither sense nor feeling. The circumstances were
peculiar, but it was none of his affair. "Send for me if
there's a need, but the danger is past. Your manservant is also on the mend."

Nicholas' first business of the day was to bring up
a truckle bed. During the day he slept when Laura
did, but a sixth sense awoke him when she stirred.
Then he got up to bring her gruel and liquids. He
took up Anton's duties, even carrying her to the
commode behind a screen in the corner. When she
cried, ready to sink with embarrassment and weakness, he made light of her shyness.

"What a goose you are. I have done some rough
campaigning on the Peninsula, you know, and am
not such a buffle-head that I cannot deal with the
needs of one sick girl." He slid his fingers into her
hair and nipped at the tip of her ear with his teeth.
She averted her head, feeling sorry for him as he
muttered softly, "I keep hoping that you will not
turn away from me." But she could not give in to his
need.

"You promised to inquire about my father while
you were away. Pray tell me if you did so. He is not
of sound mind, but still my absence must grieve
him." Laura raised her eyes pleadingly.

Touched by her distress, Nicholas replied comfortingly, "My man was able to hear at the inn in Dolton
that a Mrs. Moffitt sees to him at Danville's order."

"I am so glad! I had feared that Lord Danville
might have cut off his aid. Did you hear how he goes
on?"

But Nicholas had no intention of letting Laura know of the old man's increasing frailty. No good purpose would be served. It would probably cause her to fret the more.

"We must assume that he goes on quite well, as well as a man of his age may be expected to do. That is all I can tell you."

In two days' time Laura was able to walk around the room, feeling strength return to her limbs. But Nicholas scanned her face, seeing the shadows around the blue eyes and her pale cheeks.

"You've lost weight besides looking washed out," he observed bluntly.

"A very good reason for releasing me then," she replied.

"I may consider that in future, but not for that reason. Sick or well, in satin or in tatters, you play havoc with my emotions."

Laura backed away and smiled shyly. "Never mind that. But I have not thanked you for caring for me when I was sick."

"You may save your gratitude." His voice was harsh as he stood up and reached for her, his steely fingers settling around her arm. Then she felt his mouth lower to hers in a biting, stinging search. Her heart jolted sickeningly, every nerve cringing under his touch. When his head lifted, she looked helplessly at him, and he shook her lightly, saying between his teeth, "Little fool, I can neither bear nor forbear you. Sometimes I have admired you for your virtue. At other times I could beat you for it."

She twisted and turned her head, unshed tears pricking under her lashes, and whispered, "Please, Nicholas, let me go home." He did not know that she could see only one face, and it was not his. She could never tell him that.

He let go of her and stepped back, the gray eyes curiously without light as he stood there. "'She is a woman, therefore to be won.' Is the poet wrong, Laura?"

"Yes." He heard her soft answer and straightened his elegantly clad shoulders. "I . . . I have a feeling that you can be trusted. I do have a regard for you." Her winged brows drew together in a half-frown. "You—you know that you would never wish for a permanent relationship with one woman."

"I might run tame for you. But there! Although not of the first respectability, I am not condemned by you as a complete bounder. There is hope yet, and then there is the chance that when that is gone, I may return you to Dolton as new as this morning's rose."

"And to the stares and whisperings of those who know me." She had already thought of the wretched difficulty of explaining away her absence if she should ever have the good fortune to return home.

"That had not occurred to me," conceded Nicholas slowly, the gray eyes softening with a rueful look. He took her by the shoulders then, kissing her once more. "But that is neither here nor there. I shall kill you with kindness. You must learn to dote on me." As she covered her burning cheeks with her hands, he turned and made for the door. Feeling faint, she sank into a chair. He truly believed that in becoming his paramour, he would be raising her up in the world. She shook her head.

As she stood up, there was a loud rap at the window. She caught a glimpse of a bird. It had flown against the pane. Thinking that it was injured, she went to the window but could see only the blank wall opposite. Impulsively and with the urge to help the poor creature, she made for the door. It yielded and opened. Numbly she stood there, the knob in her hand. She had not heard the key turn in the lock when Nicholas had left. For once he had forgotten to lock it.

Laura gave herself time to think. Here was a chance to get away, she thought tremblingly. From the cupboard she drew a hooded cloak of twilled sarcenet. Again she stopped to think. She had no money. Her eye fell on the box containing the pearls. How she hated to do it, but she put them into the pocket of the cloak and quietly opened the door.

A straight carpeted staircase led down from a landing. Her soft slippers made no sound, but she held her breath at each step. She was in the lower hall. What an ugly little house it was, except for her room. She heard voices in the rear of the house. Nicholas' was not one of them. Perhaps he had gone out and was even now in the street and would see her. A glass-paned door led to the outside, and she opened it cautiously. A large woman carrying a load of baskets passed by, and pulling up her hood, Laura dashed in front of the woman, hoping that she was hidden from anyone in the house.

It would not do to attract attention by running, but she could not have done so in any case. Her legs were still too weak. It all seemed too easy, she thought. People garbed in plain, simple clothes came and went, and Laura noted that this was not a part of town frequented by people of Nicholas' stamp. At the corner she stepped quickly around a fruit vendor's stall, its buxom owner intent on counting oranges. Laura turned right. At the next corner she turned left. The streets here were lined with houses similar to the one in which Nicholas had kept her. Continuing the zigzag course, she came finally to a larger avenue lined with shops.

Ready to drop with weakness and confusion, she leaned against a wall. How was she to go on? she wondered, the sounds of the street growing dimmer in her ears. If only she felt her usual self, she could have walked or run for hours. She could have made her way out of London on foot.

A man's shape loomed up beside her, a tricorne hat set aslant above a lean, lynx-eyed face. "Having trouble, miss? Here, take my arm. Jed's the name." He surveyed her pale features with odious satisfaction.

"Th-thank you, no." Laura pushed herself away from the wall and made her legs carry her along the street. At the corner she glanced back; the man's thin shape followed a few paces behind. Desperately she pushed open the nearest door. Faintness made her dizzy, but she saw that she had entered a draper's shop. Bolts of fabric on tables and shelves rose up before her. With an effort she held herself upright, but was forced to lean against the closed door for support. She prayed that her pursuer would not follow her inside.

"May I help you, madam?" A short middle-aged man came forward and looked at her over his spectacles, his manner prodigiously civil.

"I would like to rest. Someone—a man is following me." Laura was breathless.

"He won't enter here," said the proprietor, proffering a chair. Laura sank down gratefully, allowing her head to fall against the chair back and closing her eyes. "If you will loosen your cloak, you will soon feel better, miss," he suggested discreetly.

Laura did so, puzzled at the deference in his attitude. Then the realization hit her that she was not in servant's garb. Her dark cloak was made of a fine supple material edged with braid. The lace-trimmed handkerchief in her hand was of the finest linen. Her elegant high-necked walking dress was a new one of dark-blue muslin ornamented around the hem with paler-blue embroidery. Now if she could only act the great lady, she thought, she might stay here long enough to gain strength.

"My maid is unwell and could not attend me today," she improvised. "I—I expect my carriage shortly."

"To be sure, ma'am." The proprietor bowed, all eagerness to please. The shop bell rang then, and the door opened to admit a young woman in a poke bonnet and a gray cloak. There was an abrupt change in the proprietor. "There you are, Drusilla. Make haste. The lady here bean't up to the mark. Fetch her a cup of tea."

The young woman curtsied and disappeared into the back of the shop, untying her bonnet as she went.

"You are very kind," said Laura, anxious to be hidden from anyone who might come in. "Oblige me by allowing me to rest in the back of the shop until my coachman appears."

"Certainly, my lady. This way if you please."

Laura followed his stocky figure to the cubicle in the rear, dimly aware of the tables and shelves that she passed, spread with ready-made items of gloves, hats and bonnets, lace trimmings, and ribbons. The shop was well-stocked.

"The young miss is still a trifle twitty, Drusilla," said the draper, pushing aside a curtain. Behind it, the brown-haired assistant meekly set a tray on a worktable.

"Yes, sir. I have the tea ready, Mr. Murdoch." The girl's voice was as colorless as her appearance.

Mr. Murdoch urged Laura to a straight chair, and

she sat down, giving him a grateful smile. The shop
bell sounded then, and he excused himself, telling
Drusilla to be on the lookout for the lady's carriage.

Laura drank the hot tea, feeling a little better by
the moment. Drusilla had turned her back to sort a
box of ribbons. Even from this view she gave an
impression of habitual self-effacement. Then the girl
turned and looked at Laura for an instant from a
pair of bright brown eyes. Laura smiled, unaware of
how captivating and irresistible that smile was. The
girl smiled fleetingly in return.

"Thank you for the tea. Would you not have a cup
with me?"

"Oh, no, miss. It's not allowed. I'll be havin' mine
late in the afternoon."

Laura engaged the girl in conversation and slowly
uncovered a few facts. Drusilla regarded Mr. Murdoch as something of a despot, but jealously guarded
her position, a step up from her former post as
underling in a baker's shop. She confided that only
twice had Mr. Murdoch reviled her as a clumsy
ninnyhammer. She had studied the wares until she
had memorized the entire stock, she stated proudly.

Laura felt an urgency to be gone. Mr. Murdoch
had looked behind the curtain inquiringly. She
could not prolong her stay. At her wit's end as to
what to do next, and having conceived a liking for
Drusilla, Laura made up her mind to confide in the
girl.

"I do not own a carriage, Drusilla. I told that to
Mr. Murdoch to throw him off the scent. I was
feeling so ill when I came in. I pray you, don't look at
me in such an unbelieving way. It's true." Drusilla
had turned from her task and stood arms akimbo,
facing her.

"What be the matter with you, ma'am? Ye don't make good sense."

"I don't, do I? This is all I have in the world besides the clothes I stand up in." She took the pearls from her pocket. They glowed and shimmered in her palm.

Drusilla stared and shook her head disapprovingly. "Stolen, be they?"

Laura saw that she was about to be taken to task by the girl. She must tell her the whole story and hope to make herself believable. And she must tell it in a hurry before Mr. Murdoch reappeared.

"No, they are a gift to me, Drusilla. My station in life is lower than yours. I am a servant in the country home of the Earl of Danville. His mother, my beloved Lady Danville, who is now dead, took me in hand and taught me many things."

Drusilla shook her head and looked at her incredulously. "Well, now, miss, I can smell out a hoax as well as the next. Don't look likely."

But when Mr. Murdoch appeared from around the curtain at that moment, she kept her silence, Laura saw with relief.

"Ye're better, ma'am?" When she smiled and assured him that she was, he vanished again.

"What's to do now, miss? Ye can't be stoppin' here."

"I know that, but I want to tell you how I came here. Drusilla, I have no one to talk to, and I must seek your advice."

"Sounds like a hum to me." And with that discouraging remark, Drusilla returned to her sorting. Laura persisted, telling of how she had been abducted and taken prisoner, and how she had escaped. She spoke hurriedly, unwilling to give any intimate details, but her sincerity impressed Drusilla. The girl turned and listened to every word.

"If that don't beat all. It do seem like a Banbury tale, but I be halfway taken in. I can see why the men be wanting to squire you about. How did ye come by the pearls?"

"The man who kept me prisoner bought these clothes and made me accept the pearls. I had no money. I took the pearls, thinking to pawn them. I swear I will return them or repay him in some way. I must get home to my father, who is old and ill, even though I will be held up to some shame by everyone there because of my disappearance."

"Pawn the pearls? How? Ye're green as grass, miss. Ye don't know beans when the bag is open."

"Maybe you could tell me, Drusilla."

"As to that, I don't know from nothing, neither. I don't deal with such goings-on."

"Do you believe what I've told you?"

"It's a hocus-pocus you tells, miss, but ye don't seem trickish."

"I have told you the truth. Please help me, Drusilla."

"There's a storage room upstairs." Drusilla spoke slowly and uneasily. "You can stay up there awhile. After Mr. Murdoch leaves, I stays to clean up shop."

"Oh, Drusilla, you are an angel." Laura went to her and dropped a kiss on her cheek.

Drusilla seemed surprised. "Quick, up the steps now. Mr. Murdoch'll take it that you left by the side door."

When Laura entered the little room upstairs, she sank to the dusty floor, leaning forward to support her head on a wooden box. She had no need to try to be quiet. In relief and exhaustion, she was asleep in a minute.

Downstairs Drusilla continued her work in the back room, undecided and wondering what she should say to Mr. Murdoch. She was not to have time to think. Suddenly the curtain parted and Mr. Murdoch appeared, followed by a rough-looking character in servant's livery whose eyes darted around the room.

"She ain't here," he said to the proprietor in an accusing tone.

"So I see," replied the shop-owner. "Where is the lady, Drusilla?"

"Why, she looked out the door and said that her carriage had pulled into the side street, sir. Then she thanks me and leaves." Drusilla's eyes did not waver from her employer's. Neither he nor the servant could detect the rapid heartbeats under her blank look.

"Happen it's not the moll I'm on the hunt fer, and happen it is. But I'm out this door to see if I kin smoke her out." He paused. "Master's offered ten guineas to the lucky bloke what finds her or the pearls she snaffled. But it ain't so much the pearls he's lookin' fer," he leered as he flung himself out the side door.

Toward dusk Drusilla came into the upstairs room to rouse Laura, still soundly asleep. When Drusilla took her by the shoulder, she stumbled to her feet, her legs so stiff that she could barely stand.

"I'm sorry to be so light-headed, Drusilla. I will be better directly. Thank you for allowing me to rest."

"After you wash down these rolls with tea, ye'll come about, miss. Sit ye down on the box there." Drusilla displayed a tray on which rested three large rolls stuffed with boiled beef and two mugs of tea.

Laura sat down and ate ravenously. Again she

thanked Drusilla for taking care of her so handsomely.

"Well-a-day, miss, I've come to believe you, seein' as a rough-lookin' customer barges in while you be asleep. Gives out he's lookin' for a swell lady and a pearl necklace. When I let fall to him and Mr. Murdoch that ye had left in a carriage, he's out the side door after ye quick as a flash."

Laura shuddered with relief. "I'll pray that I can return your goodness to me this day, Drusilla."

"Twarn't nuthin'. But the notion of fobbing off some pearls don't stand a chance now, miss." At Laura's hearty agreement, Drusilla went on. "If ye look down at yer gown, ye'll see I cut off twelve pearl buttons while ye slept. Mr. Murdoch gives me a few buttons now and again, and I sells them at the button shop. I got a few shillings fer them good buttons. That be why we had supper and some left over. Now, while I does the cleaning, ye can sew on these old buttons I fetched up." Drusilla lit a candle and left Laura to the task.

As she sat there sewing, Laura looked around her at the dingy storeroom. Would Drusilla allow her to stay the night here? Oh, if only she would agree to that.

When Drusilla returned, it was dark, and past time for her to return to the two rooms she shared with her parents and sister. After Laura's earnest promise to be very quiet both night and day, Drusilla agreed to let her stay above the shop for a time, until they could devise a plan between them for Laura to return to Dolton.

"Which you'll pardon me for sayin' is a ragtag notion. It's plain ye'll be pushed into a corner by all as knew ye there, what with the rare tale ye'll have to tell that nary a soul will believe."

"I won't have an easy time of it."

But she must go back to be with her father. Glendon and its master did not bear thinking on. She was sure that the earl had made short work of her in his thoughts. Having taken into consideration his mother's affection for her, he would now feel that he had discharged every obligation his family owed her. This was especially so, since she had taken a resolve not to involve Nicholas Venner. In many ways he had acted the part of the gentleman. He had not forced her compliance, which he could easily have done. To accuse him could only cause trouble. She would probably not be believed, anyway. Still, she must think of some explanation for her absence. She was too tired now to think, but before she reached home, some half-likely tale would come to mind.

15
CHAPTER

Laura awakened very early in the morning of her second day in the draper's shop. She was sustained by six hard-boiled eggs, a supply of buns, tea, and three oranges supplied by Drusilla, who stated that she still had two shillings left from the sale of the buttons. Drusilla had also brought her a pitcher of water and a bar of soap. At night Laura slept on a table, using her cloak for a cover and a folded length of sheepskin for a pillow, and listened to the scuttling of mice between the walls. Mr. Murdoch had not ventured upstairs, and she was hard put to keep perfectly quiet in the daytime until Drusilla brought her a book from below, *A History of Eighteenth-century Fashion.* Now, long before either Mr. Murdoch's or Drusilla's arrival, she broke out of her prison long enough to explore the downstairs.

The shop was a large one, and Mr. Murdoch had added merchandise not commonly seen in a linen-draper's shop. Laura was fascinated by the ladies openwork stockings and a tray of enamel brooches priced at half a crown. There was even a children's corner holding books like *Why Whip Poor Will* and *The Book of Frogs and Lily-Pads,* and boxes of paints for twopence. Inside a glass case were mouth-watering yellow sugar bunnies and striped cinnamon candies.

Far back in a corner of a shelf, Laura espied a peculiar bonnet. An idea came to her as she looked at it, and she took it down to try it on. It was dusty, and made of brown merino wool. A long shovel-shaped brim extended at least ten inches in front and at the sides of her face. Around the bottom was attached a cape about a foot wide, so that the wearer's neck would be protected from the weather. She had never seen such a quaint and unusual headdress. Putting it back, she retreated to her hiding place, anxious for Drusilla's arrival and her opinion of the notion she had just conceived.

Drusilla entered, carrying a bag evidently holding food for the day, and Laura said eagerly, "Drusilla, I have the cleverest idea of how to disguise myself!"

"Not before we eat, miss," replied the practical Drusilla dampeningly, instructing Laura to set out the buns and a small jar of honey, while she herself went below for the tea tray.

Over their breakfast, she recalled at once the bonnet Laura had espied below. "Why, that be a bonnet Mrs. Blythe brought to Mr. Murdoch, thinkin' there might be a call for it sometime. She be a Quaker, strict in her notions. There be a few of them living near. No ribbons or embroidery. The women wear dark bonnets and capes. Mrs. Blythe be a Friend, she says. They be good, kind people."

"Well, I know nothing about them, to be sure, and I may be a shuttlehead, but could I not disguise myself as one? Although," she laughed, "I did try on the bonnet and thought it dangerous. One looks out as if through a tunnel."

Drusilla thought for a moment, her bright brown eyes serious. "Mayhap," she finally admitted. "Mr. Murdoch might sell me the bonnet dog-cheap. It 'ud

keep that bonny face hidden, I'll warrant. If we could
cover ye up with Quaker clothes, ye might fob folks
off. Ye might carry a hymn book, too."

"Famous!" Laura clapped her hands. "Drusilla,
you are a treasure and an angel!"

"Sh! Mr. Murdoch be due. Now, sit ye here quiet
while I puts me mind to it today."

At the evening meal it was decided that the idea
might be possible. Laura was sure that Nicholas and
his people would still be on the lookout for her,
especially on the road that led to Dolton. Dolton
would be "un-come-atable" unless Laura disguised
herself.

"Every loose fish on the way would be casting
sheep's eyes, what with you bein' so easy to look at,"
asserted Drusilla. "Tonight I'll be takin' your dress
to a hand-me-down stall. It'll fetch a good price and
mebbe I kin find a dress and cape to match that
bonnet. Mrs. Blythe wears a one-piece dress and a
cape tied at the waist."

"Take my petticoat and cloak also, Drusilla. The
petticoat is trimmed with Brussels lace. But keep a
sharp eye out for anyone watching. I could not bear
for you to take a risk for my sake."

"Never mind that, I knows me way around, miss.
Now, take off yer clothes and I'll fetch a cover to pin
on you till mornin'."

In the morning Drusilla brought a large package.
Inside was a shapeless black dress and a three-
cornered black shawl. Her serious face beamed as
she produced eight shillings and laid them on the
table. Laura put on the oversized dress, wincing at
its unwashed odor. Drusilla adjusted the cape, criss-
crossing two ends of it and fastening it at the waist.

"It is not becoming, but at least it will be warm,
and the hood will be a great advantage if it rains.

How fortunate I am, Drusilla, that I happened into this shop."

"That's as may be. You be'an't home yet. Today I asks Mr. Murdoch to sell me the bonnet. This evenin' I draws a map of how to get out of London."

But that evening Drusilla had another plan. "Ye think Dolton is off the Bristol road. Then we might take a chance at the market. Farmers be bringin' victuals in. Mebbe some be comin' from Dolton way. Tomorrow's a market day, and we'll give it a try-on."

Drusilla came for her in the early morning, and the two made their way to the market, where farmers arrived before dawn to set up their stalls of vegetables, live chickens, pies, cakes, fish, and homemade items. Even though Laura held tightly to Drusilla's hand, she was still jolted and elbowed in the crowd because of her narrow field of vision under the bonnet. Several apologized for their clumsiness, and Laura realized that her manner of dress was regarded with some respect by the passersby. One small boy planted himself in front of her and had a good look at her face.

"Why, she be'an't an old granny, Ma. Hers got a flower face."

Laura lowered her head and turned aside. She waited patiently while Drusilla held a conversation at several stalls, inquiring in a friendly way whether the proprietors might have come from Abington way. One farmer pointed out such a person, and Drusilla led her on. At the appointed stall, Drusilla began to discuss the price of a cabbage head with the farmer's wife. One peek from under her bonnet at the fat red face of the woman convinced Laura that she was a kindly soul.

"Nary a worm in that, ye'll seldom see such a good stiff head."

"Ye can bundle it up fer me. Now, did I hear your neighbor across sayin' ye folks were from Abington? Me father's folk farmed north of there."

"Our plot's east of Abington, had the living there fer always, on Squire Manson's land, my husband's family did," stated the woman proudly.

Drusilla nudged Laura to move away, and Laura could hear little of their talk until a loud bluff voice erupted, evidently that of the farmer himself. "Well, now, missy, if ye wanted a ride yerself that's one thing, but that queer female you has there is another."

"She be quite respectable, of the Quaker faith she be, devoted to good works," said Drusilla firmly.

"Effen she kin see to do it," he laughed.

"There is no need to snigger at someone who be strong in her belief," rebuked Drusilla.

Now we're for it, thought Laura, but Drusilla must have shown him some money. The farmer now said slowly, "Weel, fer that she kin ride as far as the turnoff to me farm. We'll be leavin' in the afternoon when me cabbages is sold off."

"She'll be here waitin'," promised Drusilla, returning to Laura and taking her by the arm. "Ye'll have a long wait. The safest place be the church two blocks away. Now, look to see where the stall be, and watch as ye go so ye kin make yer way back." Drusilla stopped at an embrasure near the bronze doors of an old church, placed a small package in Laura's hands, and gave her a coin purse.

"Here be all the money that's left, and something to eat. I gave the farmer two shillings, they's honest folk. I have to go to the shop now. When the church opens, ye kin stay there until time to go back."

"With this bonnet I can't kiss you properly,"

exclaimed Laura tearfully as she took Drusilla's hands in hers and brought them to her lips.

"Now, miss, no need to fuss yourself," rebuked Drusilla. "Good luck to ye."

"I have your direction. I will do you a kindness yet," promised Laura, her voice still tearful.

"God will watch over ye. Good-bye."

Drusilla pressed her hand and was gone, leaving behind her a warm feeling of comfort. Laura lost sight of her down the street. It would be wonderful if she could someday improve Drusilla's place in the world, she thought. Besides a kind heart, she had the qualities of ingenuity and courage. Education was all that she lacked, but to such an industrious person as Drusilla, that was a temporary obstacle.

The day wore on. Laura took a seat inside the church and sat in the dank atmosphere for hours. She watched an occasional worshiper and gazed at the stained-glass windows, thinking of Drusilla's goodness. When the church bell chimed noon, she ate half a roll.

The predicament of going home took possession of her thoughts. Now that it seemed she might succeed, her only place of refuge would be with her father. Nicholas would still be seeking her, she was sure, but he could not take her from her father's cottage. Or would he try? She shuddered. If she could hide herself and enter the house after dark, she might stay concealed in the loft. Her father's mind wandered. If he spoke of her presence to others, might they not take it as an old man's meanderings? Mrs. Moffitt would have to know, but she might keep silent. She would be a willing prisoner there for the sake of being reunited with her father, whom she loved dearly.

Whenever her thoughts turned to Glendon and its owner, she was filled with anxious foreboding. She owed so much to his mother and Lord Danville. Despite the disapproval and set-downs she had endured at times, she had finally risen in his esteem. Any good opinion of her he might have held had been sacrificed now with her unexplained disappearance. Laura longed to see him but feared it even more.

It was time to make her way back to the stall. Perhaps the farmer might sell out faster than he had foreseen. But he and his wife were still there, the woman grumbling at the gloomy day, which had slowed the shoppers. A drizzle had begun to fall, and Laura sat on a box the farmer indicated, grateful for her thick hood and shawl. The farmer's wife said comfortingly that they might make an early start for home.

"I be of no mind to set here in the rain all afternoon. Effen that cove comes and wants the rest cheap, ye sell them, Mr. Greet," she instructed her husband.

"Eh, well," he agreed, his cheeriness of the morning gone.

Caroline Venner stood at the window of the Venner town house looking with distaste at the dreariness of the view: the dripping plane trees and the occasional passing of a closed carriage, the coachmen huddled on the box. Usually immersed in her own feelings and desires, she was finally becoming concerned about her brother. She had always thought them cut from the same cloth, and if there was anyone she had a scrap of affection for, it was Nick. He understood her, she thought, because he was cast in the same mold. But he had changed in

the last weeks. He had no sympathy for her loss of
Danville's esteem; he had dared to tell her that she
lacked the proper tenderness of a woman, that she
might be fastidious in her outward appearance but
that her mind lacked real taste, elegance, and understanding.

"The truth is," he had said, "our parents gave us a
free hand, but not in the proper place."

"Oh, la-di-da! I was not aware that your favored
ladies are models of virtue," Caroline had replied.

Now she heard Nick's step on the stair, and he
entered with his easy air of assurance. Caroline
turned to look at him, noticing the slight hollows
around his eyes and the grim line of his jaw. He
looked that way a great deal of late, especially after
one of his sessions with Anton or after his unexplained absences at strange hours of the day or
night. His odd humors and changed habits had also
been observed by his friends, whose libertine ten-
dencies had begun to weary Nick. Only yesterday
Louisa had heard him informing one of his intimates
that the fellow had only two faults: everything he
said and everything he did.

She saw now that he was dressed to go out, his
neckcloth impeccably folded and his fine blue coat
molded to his form. "Dear Nick, you have such a
wooden countenance of late. Won't you tell me why?"

Nick cast her a measuring glance with something
of contempt in it. "I don't know what I'd do without
you, my dear, but I'd rather." Seeing that this
remark made no dent in her composure, he went on,
"I have been apprised that you have Wharton in
tow. More your style than Danville." Mr. Wharton's
birth was unexceptionable, but his habits were not.
A grandson of a duchess and not wanting for money,
he had turned his house in Pall Mall into a gaming

hall but was still regarded as a tulip of the first
stare.

Caroline twitched the skirt of her modish morning
dress and spoke in a subdued tone. "His family are of
the first consequence, and he has decided to mend
his ways."

Her brother looked surprised. "He's come up to the
mark and proposed? But you're quite wide of it if you
think to reform him. You don't harbor the bird-
witted notion that he'll suffer a sea change, surely?"

Caroline put on her righteous look. "You needn't
make a jest of it. Papa is all for it."

"I daresay. I don't wonder at that. What a clunch
you are, Caroline, that you can't see that Wharton is
a loose fish and always will be."

Incensed, she threw back her head and glared at
him. "Pray don't kick up such a dust. The matter is
settled."

"Has Danville called since you have been in
town?"

"No," she replied shortly, turning her head away.

Nicholas looked at her half-pityingly. "Well, I'll
say no more. You always did take some notion into
your head and hold to it buckle and thong. I shan't
vex you now. Perhaps later you'll see reason." With
that he sketched a bow and made his way out,
picking up his hat and caped coat in the hall.

But it was no soiree that he meant to attend. Since
Laura's escape his whole effort had been directed to
finding her. He had tracked down every lead that he
or Anton could uncover. Every day that passed made
him more restless; he was beginning to despair of
ever finding her. He was convinced that she was still
in the city, and imagination painted vivid pictures
of what might happen to a penniless girl in London.

Anton kept track of any news that might be picked

up from servants' gossip. That morning he had informed his master that an attractive lady's maid had been employed by Lady Carlton, an elderly lady who lived in one of the smaller houses in Brook Street. The description of the girl's coloring and features resembled that of Laura. But as he took the short walk to Brook Street for an early call on Lady Carlton, Nicholas's step had no spring to it. It would be just another come-to-nothing effort.

16
CHAPTER

To Laura, the journey under damp skies seemed to go on forever. She rode in the back, seated on the rough boards of the wagon, and shivered in her shawl. Little did she know that it was only the beginning of her misery. Farmer Greet and his wife were silent in the front, their only comments an occasional lackaday or a lament on the weather. Sometimes there was a driving rain, then again a drizzle. Once or twice the rain actually ceased for a spell, then began again. At one time the farmer turned and bade her drink some beer he had made. She took the jug gratefully. It warmed her and reminded her of the strong ale her father had brewed at home.

Vehicles and horses passed them, one or two of them very smart, the horses with plaited manes and docked tails. Sometimes they passed through wooded areas. Laura saw in her narrow vision groves of lime trees and low-sweeping firs.

Night fell and the rain continued. The farmer's wife handed her an apple and a soggy scone. Hours passed and Laura dozed, her body adjusting to the jolting of the wagon. She awoke to the sound of the farmer's voice.

"This be our turnoff, miss, and still dreggy it is. Ye may stop with us a spell effen ye have the mind."

"You are good, but I am anxious to get on. Can you direct me, pray, how to get to the villages of Dorsey or Dolton?" Laura asked.

"Why, Dorsey be north and in back of where we be. Ye've come too fur." In the dimness he shook his head at her. "Next road ahead, ye'll have to turn right and get to Suthan. There ye've to turn back east."

"Yes," agreed Laura hastily. "I planned to stop at Suthan."

"A long trek ye'll have," put in Mrs. Greet. "But there'll be the Golden Lion at Suthan. Bristol stage do stop there."

Voicing her thanks again, Laura jumped down from the wagon, carrying her small bundle. It must be midnight at least, she thought as she plodded on, taking the next road to the right. It was still raining. She walked several miles before she saw a large haystack in a field near the road. As a child she had played in haystacks and knew what a refuge they could be. She could burrow into it and find a place to rest. Carving out a hole, she backed into it and covered the opening with hay. Here it was dry and safe. Even though her clothing was wet through and stalks of hay pricked her, she fell asleep.

In the morning Laura came cautiously out of her burrow to see that the rain had stopped and that a heavy fog lay over the land. She ate a bit of the bread and sucked an orange Drusilla had given her. She shook the dust and hay from her damp clothing, checking to see that the pearl necklace was still safely sewn into the hem of the black dress. By some means it must be returned to Nicholas Venner. Her dress positively reeked, she thought disgustedly as she trudged on to what she hoped was the village of Suthan. But her sleep had not revived her. Her limbs felt heavy, and the dry cough she had had in her recent illness had returned. She met no one on the road, and finally the thatched cottages of Suthan appeared through the mist.

The Golden Lion was a prosperous place, its stables and cobbled yard large enough for a score of vehicles. This time of day was not a busy one, and so Laura came timidly to the common room, where an indifferent serving maid gave her a hot kidney pie and a mug of tea in exchange for sixpence. When Laura asked her how she might get to Dorsey, the answer was discouraging.

"Dorsey be a good spell east. There be a carriage for hire in the yard effen ye have the ready to pay fur it." She looked askance at Laura's shovellike bonnet and her unkempt appearance.

Laura could force down only half of the kidney pie. Nausea caused her mouth to fill with salt water. She gulped down the tea and hastily went out the door into the inn yard. She ran behind a wagon and proceeded to lose her lunch, leaning against the wagon until the dry heaving of her stomach stopped. I must be getting on, she thought frantically as she stood there faint and trembling. Somehow she must walk; the few coins she had left were not enough for hiring a carriage.

As Laura crept to the inn-yard entrance, a bell tinkled and a peddler's cart passed out pulled by a lanky horse. The creature's head was adorned by a large straw hat, his ears coming up through two holes in the brim. Laura heard his master admonishing him. "Now that be all ye gits fur ten miles, Tom. I never seed the likes, yearnin' fur food all the day, ye lazy balkin' varmint. Do yer duty and step out, there's me good critter."

Laura saw that the driver was an old man as thin as his horse. But what kind feeling there had been in his rebuke to the animal. She waited to see his direction, and when he turned east, she gathered enough energy to run after him.

"Wait. Please, will you help me? May I seek a ride with you?" Laura held out the few coins she had and looked up at him. He saw under the brim her pale lovely features and pleading look.

"Where to?" he asked abruptly.

"To Dorsey?" she questioned.

"That's where I be bound. But don't rightly know, miss," he said gloomily. "Depends on Tom here. His feet's on the ground, but some days he don't move 'em."

Laura stood patiently.

"Well, climb up, then," he said leaning over to give her a hand, then to the horse, "Now you swivel-eyed lump, git forard!"

At his stern tone, Tom began to inch along. His master kept up a flow of gruff threats mixed with honeyed words. Sometimes he cursed him up hill and down dale, and then again he praised him to the skies.

"Ye see, miss, how boneheaded old Tom be. Effen I don't keep talkin' at him, he gits hardmouthed."

"Perhaps he is hungry?" Laura offered timidly, looking at the horse's thin flanks. Her head and throat ached, but her stomach felt a little better.

"Don't ye believe it. It's me what's hungry tryin' to pay fer oats. Tom's spindly but he be a piggish eater."

Laura clung to the hard seat. Fields and trees on the way began to swim in her vision. Soon she began to sing a lullaby, but the song stopped, the words

blurring in her memory. As from a long distance she
heard the old man crooning to his horse. His voice
faded away. She was back at Glendon, seeing the
great cedars that grew on the sun-lit lawn and
among them the statue of Diana on its pedestal. Pax,
fat and playful, romped there, running around the
stone figure and trying to escape from Laura's
grasp.

"Pax," she muttered, "you bad dog!" She tried to
stand and did not feel the tinker's wiry hand pulling
her back to her seat, or see his look of concern.

"'I saw two swans of goodly hue come softly
swimming down along the Lee,'" quoted Laura, her
solemn gaze turned toward him.

He saw the glazed look in her eyes. "Where do ye
think ye be?" asked the old fellow anxiously. But she
did not hear him. She weaved back and forth on the
seat. Afraid she would fall out, he pushed her to the
floor of the cart. Her head rested on the seat. He
untied the strings of the huge bonnet. Her thick hair
was wet to his hand, and fire burned in her cheeks.

Best keep on to Dorsey, he decided worriedly,
where some good soul might help a sick girl. The
horse Tom had not rebelled yet and might be enticed
to complete the trip. But the wily Tom had gone his
length and stopped stubbornly. The tinker was
obliged to offer him his measure of oats. The old man
patiently held a pail for the horse, while Laura lay
on the wagon floor. She was lost to all sense of where
she was, and she muttered incoherently.

Around a bend in the road swept a carriage bound
in their direction. Very black and shining it was,
with a dignified-looking man on the box handling a
pair of high-stepping bays.

The tinker held up his hand. The carriage pulled

up. A face appeared at the window. The old man had seldom seen a warmer smile or a more charming face, framed in a gray bonnet edged with red braid. A quiet glance from hazel eyes covered the scene.

"Well, my man?" she asked.

The old man knuckled his forehead. "Pardon, ma'am. I be Troy the tinker. Happen I took on this girl at Suthan. She be plaguey sick."

"I see that," replied the lady. "You needn't get down," she said to the man on the box as she opened the door and stepped out. When she saw the condition Laura was in, she questioned the tinker about his passenger. He denied knowing anything about her.

"Happen she was for Dorsey and so I be, and so I 'commodated her."

"And a good turn you did," approved the lady. "But surely she mentioned some place in her talk."

The tinker thought for a minute. "Wal, she be mumblin' 'bout a dog, Pax. Then she be whisperin' she had to help her good mistress, Lady Danville. That be all I cud make of it."

"Dear me! What a rare to-do!" said the lady, a surprised look in her fine eyes. "My husband, Mr. Brandon Russell, is well acquainted with the Earl of Danville, who has an estate near Dolton. She seems to belong there. I see nothing for it but to take her up in my carriage."

"If ye says so, ma'am," replied the relieved tinker, looking doubtfully from the shabby girl to the fine carriage.

"I do say so. You can see that the girl is at a standstill and needs care." Instructing the tinker to go to the horses' heads, Mrs. Russell beckoned to the coachman, and between the two of them they managed the task of getting Laura into the carriage. She had become a deadweight. Before she herself entered, the lady did not forget to press a silver coin into the hand of the old man.

Laura knew nothing of the trip in the carriage. When it stopped at the doctor's house in Dorsey, she did not hear Mrs. Russell's instructions that he was to follow in his gig to Glendon. Laura was propped in a corner, and it was fortunate that she did not know of their arrival there. Had she been aware of it, she would have trembled like an aspen leaf. It was the last place to which she would have chosen to come.

When the Russell coach pulled up at the entrance, Yeats opened the great doors as usual, and a footman came hurrying to open the carriage door and let down the step. Mrs. Russell had visited at Glendon several times, although her husband was the more frequent caller. When Yeats was told to send for another footman, word of Mrs. Russell's arrival reached the ears of Mrs. Meers, and she came to offer a proper welcome. When the faithful lady saw the servants carrying Laura up the stone steps, her heart gave such a lurch that she was hard put to it to stand upright. At the same time Mrs. Russell observed that the impressive exterior of Yeats was beginning to crumble. His cheek twitched nervously, and his mouth opened and closed, reminding her of a landed fish.

"It—it is Laura, Mrs. Meers," he finally got out.

"Heaven be praised, it's me chickabiddy!" breathed Mrs. Meers thankfully.

Surprised to see them so disturbed, Mrs. Russell brought them to attention by saying firmly, "And a very sick girl she is. The doctor from Dorsey will be here soon. Direct the footmen to take her to bed,

Mrs. Meers." Mrs. Meers bobbed a curtsy and hurried after the servants. "Is your master at home, Yeats?"

"No, ma'am," replied the butler, at last remembering his bow. "The earl is in London."

"Who is the girl?" asked the lady curiously.

"Laura Adams, ma'am. She was—she was favored by Lady Danville. When she disappeared, his lordship had a search set up for her."

"I may assume, then, that I have done the proper thing in bringing her here?"

"Yes, indeed, Mrs. Russell. The master will be informed of her return."

In his first examination of Laura, the doctor spoke assuredly of the immediate relief his medicines and recommended treatment would bring to the patient. He was punctual in his second day's visit, but declared himself disappointed in his hopes. The fever continued, and most of the time Laura lay in a stupor. Mrs. Meers, who had not slept all night, begged that he call in further advice. It was unnecessary, he said brusquely. He had other remedies and cordials at hand that were to be tried. It was a stubborn case. Evidently the patient had suffered an earlier illness, and exposure to the elements had brought a severe setback. Meanwhile, Mrs. Meers was to share the bedside vigil with others, he instructed grimly.

"You have a plenitude of servants standing about with their hands in their pockets. Have trustworthy people sit with her around the clock. It will be a long time before the girl can stand on her own two feet."

Mrs. Meers did as he said, but she herself took the late-night shift, anxiously watching the labored breathing and wiping the perspiration from the hot forehead. On the fourth morning, Laura's sleep became more disturbed. Suddenly she awoke, crying out with feverish wildness.

"I beg of you to hide me. Let me hide here with you!"

Mrs. Meers saw that she was not herself, and soothed her, feeling for her rapid pulse. Toward morning the housekeeper imagined that she saw a slight improvement in her breath, her skin, and her lips. The arrival of the doctor brought assurances that the patient was materially better, and Mrs. Meers was filled with joy.

"When she awakens, she will probably know you. Calm her fears, keep her quiet, and watch over her. There is always a possibility of a relapse."

And so when Laura opened her eyes, she saw the dear familiar face of Mrs. Meers. She feebly pressed the housekeeper's hand, but then a realization of where she was came to her. A look of horror dawned in her face, and she turned her head away, saying weakly, "No, it cannot be that I am here. I cannot stay. I must go, Mrs. Meers."

Mrs. Meers' reassurances could not quiet her; her head continued to move back and forth, and her breathing took on a raspier sound. Only after a strong sedative was administered did she settle down to sleep. The next day the doctor's grave looks confirmed that the patient was no better. The fever had risen, and only the laudanum kept her from restlessly tossing and turning.

Lord Danville, clad in elegant black silk, raised his foot to a velvet footstool and contemplated a narrow silver shoe buckle. Then he leaned back in the winged chair, his eyes on the small fire in his sitting room. He looks at ease, thought Beccles, his pleased and devoted valet, as he placed a tray at his elbow. He is not strung on his usual tight wire, he thought, hating to disturb him in his unusual repose. It was a change from the hammer-and-tongs pace he had been setting himself in London.

"Your pardon, sir. There is a gentleman caller below."

"Who?"

"Mr. Nicholas Venner, my lord."

Danville's dark eyes remained on the fire. It was odd, but he had seen little of Nick lately.

"Show him up, Beccles, and make ready for an early departure for Glendon in the morning."

When the door opened and Beccles bowed Nicholas in, Danville could not help but notice a subtle alteration in his friend. His big shoulders fitted his coat of yellow velvet to perfection, his hair was newly cut in a Bedford crop, his stance was as full of lazy self-confidence as always. But there was a certain languid droop of his hooded lids, and the look in the deep-set eyes was somehow devitalized.

"You're dressed for going out, apparently," commented Nick. "I shan't keep you long, Fitz."

"Devil a bit," replied the earl, filling two glasses from the decanter at his side. "You confer a benefit by lingering, actually. I am bound for some infernal ball or other that I would as soon miss. Sit down."

"I would as lief stand, if you don't mind." Nicholas seemed oddly on his guard. "You are having a deal of remodeling done belowstairs," he went on abruptly, seeming to ignore his host's gesture toward the goblet of wine.

"Only for want of something better to do. And very fortunate it has proved," acknowledged the earl. "Behind the paneling in the drawing room the workmen discovered a painting in oils painted di-

rectly on the walls. A street scene, possibly done by
Hogarth. The colors are as fresh as the day it was
painted."

Nicholas looked indifferent and abstracted, seeming not to take in the significance of the words he
heard. One of Danville's dark brows tilted as he
looked inquiringly at his guest.

"Woolgathering, Nick?"

"Eh? Not at all." Nicholas reached up a hand to
explore the hard bones of his face.

"Blister it. Are you bosky?"

"No," denied Nicholas, looking displeased. "Not
that I don't think it a good idea. The whole thing is
past all endurance, devilish awkward." His hand
rubbed the back of his neck.

"Take up your glass, sit down, and drain it,"
advised his host.

"Wouldn't dream of it, old fellow. Very improper of
me. When you hear me out, you'll be so taken in
affront that you'll likely throw it in my face and then
call me out. I'll join my sister Caroline in your bad
books."

Astonished, the earl rose to stand before the white
marble chimneypiece, his arms akimbo. "You've
windmills in your head. I have always esteemed you
for your strong sense and refined taste. As for
Caroline, I saw her briefly at Almack's and expressed my happiness for her in her upcoming marriage."

Nicholas' features twisted in a wry grimace, and
he shrugged. "I'm inclined to think that misfortune
attends the Venners in affairs of the heart. It is so in
my own case, and that is why I am here."

"What the plague have I to do with it?"

"You know the girl, and as a matter of fact, she is

under your protection. Laura Adams, the maidservant."

A swift shuttered look came over the face of the earl, veiling his thoughts. He leaned his elbow against the mantelpiece. "And what have you to do with her?" he asked carefully.

"I intend to tell you. To be frank, I am on the rack with worry over the distress and misery she may be suffering. She is somewhere in London without funds. You have had a search set up for her. If you have had any success, for pity's sake be free with me and tell me. I dote on the girl." Gone was the usual suave, cynical Nicholas. The intent gray eyes fastened on the earl were filled with raw pain.

For electrically charged seconds Danville regarded him narrowly from under menacing brows. "You may assume your customary impassive air," he announced sardonically. "She was returned to Glendon by Evelina Russell, who happened on to her on the road to Dorsey from Suthan."

A look of heartfelt relief flooded Nicholas' countenence. "Is she unharmed?" he got out.

"The only reason I let you know is because you look all to pieces. The girl suffers from exposure but will come about, evidently. Naturally, she is in no condition to be questioned. But you are, confound you. Oblige me by telling your part in this hey-go-mad affair," he ordered, a muscle tightening in his jaw, his nostrils arching in thinly veiled anger. "It is clear that I have been neatly gulled."

"It is no tale of chivalry that I have to confess," owned Nicholas candidly, calmness masking him again, "but some belated conscience compels me to lay before you all the facts. I do not fear to sink in your good opinion, although I have valued it. I now view with distaste my past follies and wicked devices. For a long time my eye was taken up with the matchless beauty of Laura's person, despite her lowly position. You know by now that Caroline and I had always a violent, headstrong will, never tempered by a parent's restraint. In short, I yielded to temptation. What of it? I said to myself. The girl is healthy, she's clean, and she's pretty. What more can a man ask? I let suspicion fall on Greystan and abducted Laura."

For a moment a dark anger erupted in the dark eyes of his host, but he leashed his temper and replied with icy smoothness. "And in abducting her you seized her from my lawful custody. But continue with your story."

"I deserve your abuse. I took her to an obscure house I had previously purchased; a room had been furnished for her. There she stayed until she escaped, and only Anton, my servant, and I entered the room."

"Do go on and omit no details," ordered Danville between clenched teeth, his expression grim.

"I plied her with words and with every blandishment, as well as with fine food, silks and satins, and jewelry. Laura would not yield to me. There is a quality of native propriety about her. I could not forfeit my honor by forcing her. I have never seen a girl like her." Self-derision pulled at Nicholas' mouth, and a flicker of pain crossed his face.

"Well, I'll be damned."

"Probably. It is eight days since I left her door unlocked and she escaped. You have no notion of what anxiety I have been in."

"Have I not? It is a deal longer than that since she was taken prisoner." Danville began to pace the room, suppressed anger in the set of his shoulders.

Suddenly he turned on Nicholas. "Damned rake-hell!" His voice was guttural with rage as his powerful right hand bunched. Nicholas saw too late the smoldering darkness in his face. Danville's fist connected and flattened him with such force that Nick found himself stretched full length on the carpet. His head ringing, he looked up to see the glowering earl standing over him. "I should thrash you to ribbons."

Nicholas raised himself on one elbow and rubbed his jaw, where a dark bruise began to appear. "I assumed you would go for the wineglass instead of planting me a facer," he complained reproachfully.

"Oh, get out before I plant you another," returned the earl disgustedly, going to stand before the mantel, his back to the room.

There was a long silence while Nick got to his feet and brushed himself down. "Is it pistols at dawn?" he asked finally.

"No," Danville answered without turning his head.

"I'll take my leave, then." His host heard him making for the door, but as it opened, he turned in the opening. "One more question, Fitz. I am curious. Why do you not call me out? Is the affair of too little consequence?"

Danville turned, still rigid with anger. "You mistake the matter entirely. I'll not have a devil of a dust kicked up, with speculation rife in every drawing room," he stated in arctic accents.

"Yes, well, quite cockle-headed of me," admitted Nicholas, sketching a bow before he closed the door.

17
CHAPTER

Glendon was a welcome sight, the sunlight making the turrets and windows glisten. Danville rode up the long slope to the house, the brightly colored leaves that had fallen dulling the hoofbeats of his tired horse. There was a nip in the air. It had whetted his appetite, and he meant to ask for a snack of Dutch cheese and ale while he glanced over the mail. As soon as he drew up at the door and slid from the saddle, Beccles and a mounted groom following, the ponderous form of Yeats opened the heavy door. Two footmen stood to attention behind him. The butler relaxed his self-imposed restraint to utter a thankful "Praise be you are at home, my lord."

The earl pulled off his gloves and raised his brows at this out-of-character comment. "What the devil, Yeats? You look as if you are contemplating suicide."

Yeats endeavored to restore his features to rigidity. "We fear for Laura, sir. She is sinking."

"What's that you say? Word was sent to me in London that Dr. Graham pronounced her not seriously ill." Danville looked accusingly at the butler, forgetful of the glove half off his hand.

"Since then the disorder has increased considerably, Dr. Graham reports, my lord."

"Send Mrs. Meers to me," instructed his master

crisply, entering and walking toward his study. But a new resolution took him, and he turned toward the staircase in a rapid ascent, the footmen staring and Yeats failing to reprove them.

Up he went to the top floor. He knew where Laura's room was. When he turned the knob, he stopped for an instant, almost as if hesitating to enter. Mrs. Meers was there, bent over the bed and laying cool cloths on the girl's forehead. He advanced to the bed and saw her form beneath the covers, still as stone, the features gaunt and the blue veins visible beneath the skin. Mrs. Meers looked up in surprise and straightened wearily when she saw him.

"What is it with the girl?" he asked in a husky undertone.

"I could have swore she was better, sir. She knew me plain; she knew where she was; she said she could not stay, or some such foolishness. Then suddenlike she were taken in a bad way."

"What does Graham say?"

"He said today he be apper—appre—he be—"

"Apprehensive?"

"Yes, sir. He be afeared about her lungs."

"Fetch pillows, Mrs. Meers." When the woman supplied thick pillows, he propped Laura higher in the bed.

"Now fetch liquids and weak gruel. We must somehow get her to eat."

When the housekeeper returned and saw her master still at the bedside, she could not hide her astonishment. "At the doctor's orders Tess be waiting to sit with her, sir. Doctor be havin' her tended the clock around."

"Dismiss Tess. As for you, get some rest, Mrs. Meers. I will speak with Dr. Graham when he comes." He settled in a chair beside the bed, his lips closing in a grim line.

Then began a rigorous course approved by Dr. Graham. Soup, juices, and broth were forced on Laura, often unsuccessfully. Hot and cold compresses were applied, depending on the rise and fall of the fever. At night the fever was at its worst, and Laura was taken from the bed in her blankets and rocked in a large rocking chair. She began to respond to a low voice that sometimes coaxed and sometimes scolded.

"You must get strong, else you will miss seeing the beauties of autumn and the changing colors in the woods. Today I saw a skylark standing in a ray of sun on a holly bush."

Or she distinctly heard a reproving voice saying, "You are a bad, stupid child. What a plague you are to the household; I am of a mind to scold you severely."

One night when she was conscious of being rocked back and forth, she heard a low chuckle. "Perhaps you should be taken to the spa at Worthing. It would serve you right. You would have to drink the sea water as a beverage. It is said to be antispasmodic and antibilious, you know."

It was either the compelling voice or the careful nursing that caused Laura to get better. The tightness in her chest eased, and she began to cough so hard that her ribs ached. The voice she had heard was gone, but Mrs. Meers, Tess, or one of the maids was always there beside the bed.

Mrs. Meers exclaimed to Laura over the earl's concern. "Ye should have heard the orders he's given, not to mention the times he's been in this very room to see that all's as it should be. 'No slacking," he says, 'nothing is to be left undone.' And the hours he spent on the night watch!"

"Did he—did he seem angry?" Laura was puzzling over her dim recollections of being held and rocked.

"Oh, my aunt! With ye, ducks? Why it's plain as the bump on a cottage loaf he's been in a taking over ye." Mrs. Meers was spooning brown broth into Laura's mouth. "Doctor says ye may sit in the chair a spell each day soon as ye're able."

But now Laura tried to sit up, a look of distress dawning on her face. "Oh, Mrs. Meers, the dress I wore when I came. Where is it?"

"That scrubby thing? Why, it be in the bottom of the cupboard. I should have burned it afore."

"No. Promise you will leave it there. I have need of it," Laura begged.

"Settle down, lass. It 'mazes me why you want it, but there it'll stay."

By the next week, Laura could sit in the chair, and Dr. Graham allowed her to read there every afternoon. He informed Mrs. Meers that she was to be well-wrapped and carried to the garden occasionally, where she might sit in the sun for an hour if the weather was favorable. To Laura's dismay he forbade her to do any kind of handwork.

"One day when I wake up entirely well, Mrs. Meers will be sending for you to find out what is wrong with me," she said bitterly.

"That's the lass," he approved. "Complaining is a sure sign of recovery. Right now, my orders are that whenever you feel like moving about, lie down until the feeling passes."

One morning she sat reading the comedy *The Rivals*. She had wanted to delve into her textbooks, but the housekeeper had refused to bring them.

Instead, a small stack of books from the library had been sent up, none of which could be called heavy reading. Laura wondered whose hand had chosen them. Probably it had been Dr. Graham's, but the thought that the earl himself might have chosen them caused her heart to pound like a drumbeat. I have often been in his bad books and must be more so now, she thought. She had had many proofs of his present kindness. Was he kind because of an obligation to act as his mother wished? Was he being conscientious in the performance of a duty? He must have some curiosity about what had happened to her in the past weeks. Mrs. Meers had told her that he had set up a search for her.

So far Laura had told no one about that strange and terrible time, and no one had questioned her. But she had rescued the pearls from the hem of the black dress. Somehow she would get them back to Nicholas Venner. She would never forget Nicholas. His obsession for her had caused her to grow up in a hurry, she thought wryly. She recognized that the feeling he had for her was genuine. He was a gentleman in spite of the self-indulgent life he had led. In his own way he had been generous and caring. He had benefited her, too. By resisting him she had strengthened her own self-image. She had grown up enough to face the future.

Laura was so engrossed in her thoughts that she did not hear the door open. She did hear the latch as it fell in place. Glancing up, she saw that it was Lord Danville, looking complete to a shade in a coat of pewter gray.

"You begin to look better, no longer as thin as a whisper." Laura started up from her chair. "Sit still!"

"Yes, sir. I—I am better."

"I am glad, as are all those who know you here. Yeats tells me that even the irritable head gardener asks after you."

Laura colored and laid her book in her lap. "I have caused a great deal of trouble. I—I meant to go to my father's cottage."

"I have news of your father. I must tell you that his mind becomes increasingly clouded. Mrs. Moffitt continues to prepare meals for him, and a girl from the village stays at the cottage with him." At her anxious look, he continued, "Dr. Graham tells me that he is not suffering. I daresay he lives happily in the past."

"Again I must thank you for my care and my father's, all of it due to your goodwill, my lord." She looked at her hands, one gripping the other so that the knuckles showed white.

"You embarrass yourself as well as me when you offer thanks so humbly," he observed dryly. "I have always thought gratitude a rather mediocre sentiment." He saw her stiffen in her chair.

"Mediocre?" she asked. "It is considered rare at any rate." Her look challenged him. "It is all I have to offer."

"Possibly," he agreed rather irritably. "There is also a daily inquiry about you from one of the Venner footmen." Now his dark eyes studied her intently, and he saw the hot flush that spread from chin to forehead. "You need not concern yourself about it, however. Your whole endeavor must be to regain your strength. Soon you will be able to go to the woods and gather walnuts for cook. There is a good crop this year. They peel as easily as taking off a glove."

Laura swallowed and tried to speak. His mention of the Venner household had silenced her. She

wanted to tell the earl about her recent experiences,
but he would have to know the identity of the man
who had abducted her. If he believed her story, what
would be the consequences? She had not the vaguest
idea, but she would not inform on Nicholas Venner,
whatever his sins. In the pause that ensued, the door
opened to admit Mrs. Meers, a tape measure in her
hand.

"Ah, you are ready, Mrs. Meers. You may take
Laura's measurements for several new gowns."

The housekeeper hid her surprise and bobbed a
curtsy, while Laura tried to focus on these new
unforeseen goings-on. Lord Danville had folded his
arms and now pondered her with a critical eye.

"Four gowns, Mrs. Meers. One of sprigged muslin,
one of Berlin silk that may be worn in the evening.
However, they must be of simple design, only an
occasional ruffle or border of lace. All to be tightly
buttoned at the wrist and made up to the throat.
When they are finished, let a cloak be made . . .
dark blue, I think."

"Y-yes, sir. And what of shoes and petticoats and
the like, my lord?"

"You'll know what is proper, Mrs. Meers. Attend
to it. Let the seamstress begin at once."

Laura thought she saw a sardonic satisfaction
on his face as he continued to look at her measuringly. What was in his mind? She had never even
hoped to take her former place in the house.
What did he intend for her? She found him inscrutable.

"I—I am not deserving of new gowns, my lord. I
would rather keep my old ones."

"What kind of a girl refuses new gowns, Mrs.
Meers? Does she not show an ungrateful disposition?" he asked the housekeeper wryly.

"She do be grateful, sir. She thinks she don't deserve it, that be all."

"Or perhaps she is afflicted with excessive pride." He straightened then, pinning Laura on his dark steely gaze, and opened the door. "I would prefer to see a more earnest desire to please."

"Well, my girl, fancy that, now! New gowns and all, and you splitting hairs over it with his lordship. It won't do," Mrs. Meers helped Laura to her feet and ran the tape around her waist. "Once he takes a notion, ye've got the wrong sow by the ear if ye think to change it. Stand still, now. Tess'll be coming up with cocoa and dripping toast."

By the next week, the new clothing began to appear, the housekeeper exclaiming over each piece and carefully putting it away in the wardrobe. The cut of each dress was similar, the Empire style following so snugly the lines of Laura's supple figure that Mrs. Meers expressed doubt that the style was exactly what Lord Danville had had in mind. "They be just what he ordered, but he don't know how ye've plumped out since ye've growed up. But wear 'em ye will. All the old clothes are to be given to the parish, he's ordered."

"And how am I to scrub and work in this?" asked Laura, looking down at a jonquil muslin gown with yellow satin binding stitched just under the bust and a narrow ruffle at the hem.

"Scrub and work, is it? 'No more of the work she was used to doing,' he says. 'She'll want to be busy,' I says. 'No need to think of that until the girl's restored to health,' says he, looking stiff. So don't balk, miss, is my advice. He's true as the dial is to the sun, but nobody better put him in a taking."

"And what am I to do, Mrs. Meers? Stand with my hands behind my back?"

"Ye'd better if ye know what's good for ye," replied the housekeeper glumly, knowing better than to air her own confusion as to why the master acted as he did.

Dr. Graham had now decreed that exercise would be beneficial. Laura begged that she be allowed to keep just one of her black gowns for walking in the wood. Mrs. Meers grudgingly agreed after sewing a bit of white lace at the neck and cuffs. It was warmer in the afternoons and on good days she took longer and longer walks, protected by a new hooded cloak of soft blue wool. She rarely saw the earl. He had resumed his country amusements and was often away. Laura kept to her third-floor room or to the back part of the mansion.

Her books had been restored to her, and she studied again. She had not forgotten what Mr. Gaunt had taught her. It was frustrating, though, as Mrs. Meers made sure that her candles were snuffed every night at eight o'clock. Then she would lie awake wondering when the day of reckoning would come with Lord Danville. She was well enough now. He would question her, and he would not be satisfied until he heard the full story. The thought made her heart thunder like a trip-hammer. And still she must somehow return the pearls to Nicholas Venner. She would always carry them with her in case an opportunity came, she decided.

She had asked many times to be allowed to see her father, and finally that permission came. Two mounted grooms accompanied her as she drove the gig into Dolton, both looking with hidden curiosity at her starched new gown and blue cloak. She was to have a visit of two hours, she had been told. Laura had worried so about her father, and now she dreaded to go into the cottage. He often did not recognize even the vicar, Mrs. Meers had told her. He might not know her. She thought of the many times he had lifted her down from the hay cart and brushed her off, saying, "And dinna ye find the needle today, lass?"

But he did know her. She was hardly aware of Mrs. Moffitt's cold manner and disapproval of her new garb. He had evidently no recollection that she had been gone for a long time. The cottage was clean and sweet-smelling. Her father's face was shriveled like a ruddy old apple, but he looked healthy. She had feared that he was suffering, but it was not so. He felt no pain in his dotage, and she came away relieved and more than ever under obligation to the family who had provided so well for him.

18
CHAPTER

Laura walked beside the high stone wall that
bordered one side of the estate. It was not a pleasant
day. A light mist masked the trees. She should not
have come out at all, but she had felt that she must
be by herself for a while. The earl had gone to
London three days ago. He had not even left a
message with Mrs. Meers regarding her, and Laura
felt herself forgotten. Even though she rarely saw
him, the knowledge that he was near comforted her
and somehow set the world to rights. His absence
had cast her into a depression.

How safe she felt when he was near. She could not
live far away from him, she thought, but she would
have to learn. She wished that she might be close to
him as long as she lived. Such a lovely castle in the
air was not for her. Someday he would marry.
Probably he would choose Caroline Venner, although she, along with her family, had not visited at
Glendon. Mrs. Meers had merely tucked in her
mouth and declined to answer when Laura had
commented on it.

A white streak of lightning sparked across the
dark-gray sky followed by a loud clap of thunder.
Laura jumped. The wind tore at her cloak, and big
drops began to fall. Sheets of water soon followed,
and Laura hurried to find shelter. Rain is my neme-

sis, she thought. Her cloak became soaked, and her slippers sank into the soggy ground. She came out of the copse and hurried across two open fields to a haycock. A roof supported by four rickety poles gave some protection.

The rain had washed her face to dewy freshness, and the water fell from her hair in crystal drops. She had thrown her wet cloak on the hay. To the rider who approached every curve of her figure was revealed, her soaked gown following its lines like a smooth glove. Lord Danville stopped there in the rain, his scathing glance moving from the slender waist down her tapering thighs. Laura, already chilled to the bone, went colder with dread, her nails biting into her palms. Mounted, he towered over her like a monumental figure in his oilskin cape.

Danville swung down from the saddle and slapped his horse's flank, tethering him to one of the posts. Stalking across the space that separated them as if he would like to stamp on something, he loomed threateningly over Laura. She crossed her arms protectively over herself, backing away from the unbridled fury in his eyes.

"Unprincipled little villain! You shall be confined to the house. Besides being perverse, you are as giddy as a goose." He reached for her shoulders and shook her fiercely.

She trembled, held upright only by the grip of his hands. "But I did not know—I did not know it would storm," she said dazedly, looking up into a face black with rage.

"I shall teach you not to submerge yourself in water time and again," he said grimly. "You will kill yourself."

Laura looked at him in confusion and bewilderment, her shoulders aching under the grip of his hands. Then the expression in his eyes altered as they dropped to the soft roundness of her full bosom and down the length of her long legs. "That gown is not one of those ordered for you."

"I—I did not want to ruin my good gown when I walked in the woods."

Danville was not listening. He was looking at the drops of rain that clung to her hair. He put up a finger to catch the drops on her brow and gently traced the outline of her soft lips with his wet finger. "A wet goose," he whispered, shifting her onto his left arm and bringing her close to the hard wall of his chest.

Laura felt a shy wonder, as if stepping into a new dimension where all sounds and sights were magnified. She could smell the warmth of his body and the starched odor of his cravat. Only let me stay here a moment, she thought distractedly, only a little while.

But he had laid her back on his arm, searching her face with a brooding intensity that frightened and exhilarated her. She felt his hands at her throat slowly loosening the buttons of the black dress and exposing the arch of her throat. His fingers tangled in her hair, and he jerked her head back roughly so that she was exposed all the way down to the swell of her breasts.

"You—you should not," she stammered thickly, hearing him laugh deep in his throat. His lips came down hard on the side of her neck. His mouth left a mark on her flesh when he eventually raised his head.

"You are right, but I shall," he asserted, his fingers caressing the back of her neck. Laura gripped his coat, the beating of her heart almost suffocating her. Before she knew it, he brought her down on the hay with him looming over her. In the smoldering darkness of his face, she could read that he was still in a temper.

He had shrugged off his oilskin cape, and underneath, his clothes were dry. Laura shivered with cold. He pressed her deep into the hay, holding her there until she began to feel the kindling glow of heat emanating from his warm body. He then rolled to the side and took one of her hands, seeing the dark-red crescents her nails had made in the palm. She felt his lips press against the mark, and her heart hammered. Danville reached a hand to draw her wet hair back from her forehead, a flame leaping in the unusual brilliance of his dark eyes. Her whole face turned cherry red under that look.

His head lowered to hers, and Laura felt his lashes brush her cheek. He tasted her lips slowly as if savoring a rare wine. Then his mouth came down hard on hers, probing and finding the sweet recesses of her mouth and filling her with a strange and wonderful heat. His breath was hers for a moment. He felt the quivering of her body against him, but it was not from the cold. But now she felt a chill of cold air. He had stirred and raised himself. She would not open her eyes knowing that he was standing there.

"It is going on for five o'clock," he said. "We should go."

Laura put up her hands to hide her hot cheeks, feeling resentment growing in her that he should suddenly speak so coldly. He was angry that she had gone out in the rain. It was as if he had wanted to take out his anger on her and had now spent as much time as he intended to spend on her. She

wished that she could pierce that lofty assurance of
his.

"If that is a suggestion, my lord, I daren't forget
who is making it," she flared, standing up and
refusing to take his hand stretched out to assist her.
Laura was afraid to look up at him, but when she
did, she saw him regarding her with a peculiar
half-twinkle in his eye.

"What a spitfire!" He placed the oilskin around
her and threw her wet cloak over his arm. They
made the trip home in silence with Laura perched on
the saddle in front of him, the rain coming down as
heavily as ever.

When Yeats opened the door to them, he was
ordered to summon Mrs. Meers. Danville propelled
Laura toward the library. There she blankly
watched the water make a puddle at her feet on the
pale carpet. Danville cast off his cloak and impatiently ordered her to stand near the fire.

Mrs. Meers appeared, concern written plainly on
her face when she saw the steam beginning to rise
from Laura's wet clothing.

"You may well stare, Mrs. Meers," said the earl
sardonically. "This girl is indeed a water sprite bent
on ending in a watery grave. Perhaps I mistakenly
remarked to you that she possessed wit and understanding."

"Oh, as to that, sir," said the housekeeper, finger-
ing the base of her throat nervously, "Laura do have
her head on her shoulders. But I did say to her not to
get maggoty and go out on such a day."

"You see how well she heeded you. After this, she
is forbidden to leave the house except to exercise in
the rose garden on a warm day."

"Yes, my lord." Mrs. Meers seemed in wholehearted agreement with this edict. "And shall I be sendin' for Dr. Graham?"

"Certainly. Perhaps between you, you may make her sorry for these tedious starts of hers." By this time Laura felt ready to sink. He spoke of her as if she were not there. Resentment began to stir in her.

"What with the decoction of all-heal I have at hand, it's likely we can stave off infection, sir. I'll be keepin' good tabs on her."

"Do not allow her to wheedle you. Depend upon it, the girl can talk the squirrels down from a tree. But there! Take the little witch away and get her dry."

"Yes, let us make haste, Mrs. Meers. A dry witch can better bedevil those around her," burst out Laura, the blue of her eyes stormy. As soon as she had spoken, she could have bitten her tongue.

Danville subjected her to a swift scrutiny. His mouth curved. He attempted to look indifferent, but a flicker of a smile crossed his face. "A sauce-box as well. See to her, Mrs. Meers," he ordered, dismissing them with a wave of his hand.

But when she lay warm and dry in bed, tears began to trickle between her closed eyelids. She had never in all her short life felt so defenseless. She loved him, and it was a biting pain in every nerve of her body. It seemed that she could feel the texture of his skin and the warmth of his breath as they had lain in the hay. What had been for him a moment of dalliance had been for her an awakening to a new world. He had never questioned her about her absence. It must have meant little to him. She was just a tiresome responsibility. But he was to her as her eyes and hands. She had not known that love could come on her like this, she thought, burying her head in the pillow.

The door latch clicked. Laura had no need to turn
and look. She knew it was he. Had it been pitch-
black, she would have felt his presence.

Danville approached the bed. "I have brought you
a glass of port. It should help you to sleep." He set
the glass on the table, seeing her head buried in the
pillow and hearing her stifled hiccups. His hands
were gentle as they turned her over. "This will not
do. I did not think to find a watering pot."

"You spoke to Mrs. Meers as if I were not there,"
she said accusingly.

"I can hardly be in charity with you when you do
something so mad-brained," he said slowly.

She looked up at him. "You think me a feather-
brain who is forever falling into scrapes."

"No. Most codlings take time to find their feet, and
I am persuaded that you have found yours." As he
spoke, his thumb caressed the tears from her cheeks.

"You do not ask what happened when—when I
was taken away. You—you would change your opinion then." He saw the tears fall again in a ceaseless
cataract down the young face.

"Nicholas Venner came to me and told me." Time
seemed to stop for Laura as he went on looking at
her. She could not see his face. Her throat ached
with her held breath. "I had previously come to
esteem your steadiness of character and delicacy of
principle. I have seen no reason to change that
opinion. But enough of that for now. Tomorrow Mrs.
Russell and her husband will be here for tea. You
will wish to thank her for her help when you were so
ill. Also, I am hoping that you will enjoy meeting
them." He retreated to the door.

"You—you wish me to come down for tea?" asked
the astonished Laura.

"Only if you feel equal to it. Do not disappoint us by falling ill again." She heard a thread of amusement in his voice as the door closed on him, leaving her there in a turmoil, wanting yet afraid to believe that she was not in his bad books. How was it that Nicholas had gone to him? What had passed between them? Why had she been asked to tea? And how was she to solve the vexing problem of how to return the pearls?

Either Mrs. Meers' dose of all-heal or her diet drink of dock roots had the desired effect. Laura was in good health the next day. Mrs. Meers looked with disfavor on the invitation to take tea, but finally recommended that Laura wear a plain gown of French cambric edged around the neck with a row of escalloped lace. Then, seeing that the girl was all aflutter, she made her swallow a small dose of valerian for the nerves. Next the good woman conveyed the news to an astonished Yeats, adjuring him to announce Laura properly at the drawing-room doors.

Laura came hesitantly down the broad staircase in the late afternoon. Yeats bowed and silently led her to the double doors, where his "Miss Adams, your Lordship" made her want to turn and flee. A familiar and lovely face turned to her from the sofa, where Mrs. Russell sat before the tea service. On her face was a welcoming smile. Farther back in the room near a large table stood Lord Danville and a handsome fair-haired man. They were studying what appeared to be maps or charts of some sort.

As soon as she was announced, Lord Danville came toward Mrs. Russell saying, "I hope you remember Laura, Evelina—you rescued her, you know. Mrs. Russell, Miss Laura Adams."

"Indeed I do." Mrs. Russell had risen and held out
her hand. "Come and sit beside me. I would almost
not recognize you, you know, you were so very sick."
She turned toward her husband. "Bran, this is the
young lady I told you of. Laura, may I make known
to you my husband, Brandon Russell?" Mr. Russell's
bow was all correctness and then he smiled at her.

Laura thought she had never seen a kindlier
smile. Mrs. Meers had told her that he was one who
"had something on his head besides his hat," but
Laura saw nothing top-lofty in his manner.

"If you will excuse us a moment, ladies, Russell
and I are concluding a little argument we had over
the location of some Viking artifacts he had come
upon." It occurred to Laura he might be arranging
matters so that she might have a comfortable conversation with Mrs. Russell. But he would not be
concerned about her awkwardness and discomfort in
this strange new situation, she told herself.

She sat beside Mrs. Russell, the lady declaring
that her husband was single-minded when his curiosity was aroused and that she, for one, had little
interest in digging through a brown bog to find a
leather boot and a wooden last.

"However, near there is a site of an old monastery,
and a farmer dug up a silver chalice intricately
filigreed with panels of gold and amber settings.
Brandon believes it was buried by the monks to keep
it from being plundered by the Vikings. They are
looking at maps of the area."

Laura was enthralled with this tale and with Mrs.
Russell herself. From the hall gallery she had often
seen the couple come and go, and thought them
distinguished. She thought now that they were
indeed distinguished for their kindness, their good

manners, and for the liveliness of their minds. Lord Danville's expression held none of the habitual disdain he often wore in company.

When the two men joined them, Laura was amazed to see that Lord Danville did everything that he could to further conversation between the Russells and herself. Evelina Russell told a tale about a lady who had fallen headlong into a pond, and Laura could not keep from laughing.

"I don't mean to poke fun at another's misfortune," said Mrs. Russell, looking apologetically at her husband, "but the lady is so very rigid. It was in a public park. The pond was full of duck weed. She thought it part of the walkway."

"I will allow that the lady is tightly buttoned up, so to speak," grinned Russell.

"And she was only abed one day afterward," continued Mrs. Russell, her hazel eyes crinkling with amusement.

"I would have given a monkey to have seen it. It might give her a set-down," acknowledged Danville.

When the Russells took their departure, both of them requested that they have the pleasure of seeing Laura again.

"Many young ladies who are pleasing company do not have eyes like stars to give added attraction," said Mr. Russell, bowing in his courtly way.

Lord Danville accompanied them to the door, and Laura took the chance to escape up the stairs. It was the first time she had been received in a company who were of the first stare of fashion. She hoped but could not know for sure that she had carried herself in a manner that met with Lord Danville's approval. She had enjoyed it. But the afternoon had given her hundreds of things to think about and puzzle over.

Her head ached and she begged an early night from
Mrs. Meers, reassuring her that she, Laura, had
been cordially received by the company. The per-
plexed housekeeper heard all this but concealed her
own misgivings at the topsy-turvy turn of events in
the household. What the master was about was
beyond her.

CHAPTER 19

The next day was warm, and Laura walked in the rose garden. It had been a favorite place of Lady Danville's, and Laura had often worked in it. Red roses had been the lady's favorites, and they were making a last bright showing before the blasts of winter. Laura paced up and down the paths of the walled area, stopping at the sundial and idly tracing with a forefinger the design in the weathered stone.

She thought about her changed status in the house since her homecoming. It had begun before the earl had singled her out with new attire and an invitation to tea. The servants had become cordial in their dealings with her. Perhaps it was because Harris was no longer there to turn them against her, she thought. Mrs. Meers refused to discuss the matter, merely saying repressively that the master had not cared for Harris' influence in the house and had pensioned her off.

She could not fathom why Lord Danville now seemed to smile upon her. From the first she had been under a cloud with him, and events seemed to support his disapproval. Now, to her incredulous joy and despite her disappearance with Nicholas Venner, her credit with him had risen. Would he continue to think better of her?

A shadow fell on the dial. Startled, she turned

quickly, her skirts rustling against the stonework.
Lord Danville stood near, and her head brushed
against one of the silver buttons on his waistcoat.
Thoroughly flustered, Laura jerked away. Danville's
low laugh sounded as she was brought up short. A
strand of long hair had become entangled in a
button.

"Stand still," he admonished. "A little forethought
and you would not find yourself in such a hobble." As
he freed her hair, his smile was heartening, showing
the edge of his white teeth. "What is that you have
in your pocket?"

His question struck at Laura like a lightning bolt.
She had meant to tell him about the necklace—after
she had returned it to Nicholas Venner by hook or
crook. She had been taken by surprise. She shook
her head stupidly in a negative gesture.

"Well?" he asked, his tone sharpening, increasing
her confusion. "I heard it strike against the dial as
you moved. Is it a key?"

Laura shook her head numbly.

"Your guilty air arouses my curiosity. Give it to
me." Laura heard the uncompromising note in his
voice and reached into her pocket. He received the
necklace and rolled it in his palm, the pinkish glow
of the pearls in sharp contrast to the darkness of his
skin. "A pretty knickknack, and costly, I'll warrant.
And now, ma'am, beg the question at your peril.
How came you by this?"

She looked up into his hard face, knowing that he
was aware of the fear hammering at her heart.
"Nicholas gave them to me," she whispered.

"You provide a perfect setting for pearls, I will
allow. Did you mean to keep them?" His mouth was
closed firmly in a disciplined line, but there was a
dangerous anger in his dark eyes. His free hand

came out to grip her wrist so tightly that she felt the blood to her hand stopped. He held her there. Laura made no sound. "Answer me!"

"What—what kind of false person do you take me for? I wish to return them if I can." She felt the pain of pins and needles in her hand as he eased the pressure but did not release her.

"I understand why the irresistible Nicholas gave them to you. Explain why you have them."

"I had no money in London. I had to get away, and—and thought to pawn them. You are hurting me."

"You are fortunate that I do not shake you like a duster," he grated, giving her arm a tug before he released it. "Beccles shall carry the necklace back to him today. Fortunately he is at home, laid up with a broken leg."

Laura stood silent, her head bent as she rubbed her wrist.

"Be plain. Are you not concerned at his plight?" he inquired, narrowly observing her for a reaction. "He had a carriage accident a month ago."

"I must be glad that he escaped serious hurt, my lord; that is all." She had raised her head and looked at him, her gaze anxious and open.

"Your eyes are as clear as blue lakes," he said slowly, taking her hand and brushing her bruised wrist with his lips. "You must pardon my cutting up rough. I find it difficult to keep an even course with you. Go in now. You have had enough turmoil for a while. After dinner pray come to me in the library." He stepped back in a bow, the sun picking out chestnut lights in his dark hair.

She felt his eyes on her as she moved toward the house, willing herself not to break into a run.

That evening the earl placed Laura in a leather

chair across from his in the library. He poured a glass of sherry for her, but it sat untouched on the table. She could not trust her hands to hold it steady. The afternoon had been spent in long contemplation of his reason for this evening's summons. She had sensed a gravity in his manner when he had made the request.

"Who arranged your hair?" he asked idly, smiling as the color came up in her cheeks.

"Mrs. Meers did it."

"A hidden talent of hers, then. It is charming."

Laura wore a lavender muslin gown with tiny rosettes of darker purple adorning its high collar. A ribbon to match was threaded through her thick hair.

He lifted an inquiring brow at her. "Mrs. Meers tells me that when Mrs. Russell delivered you here, you were oddly dressed. You have not told me how you escaped from London. You must have had a harrowing time."

"I—I did have a hard time, my lord, but people were kind to me."

Danville looked surprised. "You were fortunate. Because of your illness I have not asked you to tell of your experiences. Who was especially kind to you?"

"Oh, it was Drusilla! She worked in a draper's shop where I took refuge," said Laura eagerly. Encouraged by Danville's questions and by his interest, Laura related the happenings in Mr. Murdoch's shop and during her trip out of London. But when she paused, she looked anxiously at the frown between the black line of his brows. He leaned forward, his eyes on his hands between his knees.

"I—I am telling a confused story. I don't remember the last part too well because I was sick," she said placatingly.

He looked up with a faint smile. "The story is clear enough. I dislike hearing of your plight and the sufferings you had to endure. The girl Drusilla and the Greets shall both be rewarded. You must tell me how best it is to be done."

Laura looked at him tongue-tied—glad for her friends, but feeling as if she plunged deeper and more helplessly into his debt every hour.

As if reading her thoughts, Danville said gently, "I hope you will allow me the pleasure of helping them. We shall speak of it again when you have had time to think about it." Still she said nothing, and he went on. "But my reason for asking you here this evening is an entirely different one. It is time that I told you some facts about your parentage."

"But—but they are unknown," whispered Laura.

"My mother knew. Shortly before she died, she made me acquainted with the facts, and she exacted from me a solemn promise of silence. No other person knows anything of the matter. Daniel, our old coachman, knew of it, but he is dead. I was enjoined by my mother to tell you of your parentage at a time I deemed proper. That time has come."

Laura sat as if turned to a statue, her thoughts in a whirl.

"The facts are not so harrowing." The earl spoke softly. "I am persuaded that you are of so steady a temperament that you will not be struck all of a heap when you hear the story."

At these bracing words Laura sat up straighter in her chair. "I—I wish to hear it."

"I will tell you the most startling part first. You are the granddaughter of Mr. Gaunt. He is unaware of the fact."

"My—my tutor?" Laura asked incredulously. In

her mind's eye she saw the stern visage of the old man, a glint of humor in his icy gaze.

"A strait-laced gentleman, besides being a prodigious scholar. I thought it a nice turn to bring you two together, besides forcing you to stretch your mental powers." She saw a grin tug at his mouth.

Laura was conscious of resentment at this remark. "Your lordship's notion of humor is singular."

"Why? Did you not enjoy your association with him?" he asked in mock concern.

"Up to a point I did—that is, when I had an odd moment away from my books to think of it," she replied, marveling at her own temerity and anxious for him to continue.

"Oh, it was quite good training for you," he asserted heartlessly, seeming to enjoy the glare from her blue eyes he received in return. "But to go on: Mr. Gaunt's wife died in childbirth. His daughter grew up in a Spartan home. She was your mother. Her name was Letitia. Mr. Gaunt was even more uncompromising than he is now. He saw to a limited education for her. Immersed in the world of books and also at that time carrying on his duties as vicar, he had little time for her. Her life was spent in household chores and churchgoing. I have a vague recollection of her. My mother said that she was excessively shy and withdrawn. And no wonder, with the life she led."

"Wh-what happened then?" There was a painful eagerness in Laura's expression.

"Mr. Gaunt had been laid up with the flu. His daughter went to evensong on a Sunday evening. She hurried home in the dusk. Three gay blades from London, out for a weekend lark, came upon her. They had all been drinking heavily. One of them had his way with her. She was never able to throw off that experience. As for the three rakes, nothing was ever seen of them again."

"Dear heaven!" Laura's face was pale with shock. "But you said she did not recover. I—I do not understand."

"She recovered outwardly. It was the will to live that she lost. She crept home. In his illness Mr. Gaunt was even less observant than usual. Somehow she put on an appearance of leading her usual life. It was when she discovered that she was with child that she came to my mother."

"She could not have done a better thing," breathed Laura.

"Exactly so. My mother went within the hour to the church to see Mr. Gaunt. She exerted her persuasive abilities to such an extent that he agreed that his daughter could go to London for a long stay under my mother's supervision. Even he had seen his daughter's declining health. Within a few days my mother set off for London with your mother. Old Daniel was in attendance."

"She—she stayed with Lady Danville?"

"Indeed not! The secret would soon have been out at the house in town. My mother hired a small house and staffed it with Daniel and a reliable older woman. Your mother assumed the name of Mrs. Wren. It was understood that her husband had been lost at sea. After your mother recovered sufficiently from the birth, it was thought best for her to return to Dolton and her father. She had no real interest in anything, even you." He smiled warmly at Laura. "I am sorry that I know so few details. My mother was too weak for anything but an abbreviated story."

"Do you know if my mother was happy to be home?" asked Laura.

"That I cannot tell you. She lived for eight months

afterward and died of red fever. During that time you were kept at the house with the maidservant." Danville rose to lean indolently against the table, his arms crossed. "After that, at my mother's order, Daniel brought you to Dolton and placed you secretly with Sarah and James Adams. She never considered telling the truth to Mr. Gaunt."

"There—there is nothing to say, is there?" asked Laura in a helpless manner, pushing her hair back from her forehead. "What shall I do?"

"I recommend that you do just that—nothing," he advised seriously. "No good can come by telling the truth. The world's censure would fall on Mr. Gaunt as well as on you: on him for being an unnatural parent, and on you for having been born out of wedlock. As matters stand, no one can know for sure how you came into the world."

"Yes, I see what you mean," agreed Laura slowly. "It is odd that a helpless baby can be blamed for the conditions of his birth."

"Such a belief goes against all principles of justice," he said grimly. He straightened his lean length and stepped to the bell pull. In a moment the door was opened by Yeats.

"My lord?" he inquired with a bow.

"Instruct Mrs. Meers to prepare a sleeping potion for Miss Laura. Something laced with brandy, I think."

"Well, indeed, sir! May I remind you that I am no longer an invalid?" Laura's indignant words caused the imposing Yeats to poker up with displeasure at this piece of impertinence. Amusement flickered in Danville's eye, but Yeats heard only his curt tone.

"Well, Yeats? About it, man! Have Mrs. Meers take it to Miss Laura's room at once."

As the door closed on Yeats, his lordship turned to

Laura. "I will not have you lying awake and making yourself miserable over past history. Oblige me in this!" He stood there unmoving, ready to bow her from the room.

He would not let her go until she submitted, she thought irritably. The interview was over.

"You carry us all with a high hand, as usual, my lord," she said mutinously as she left the room.

Laura stood in front of the study doors, hesitant to enter. How she had formerly dreaded opening those doors. She remembered the set-downs she had received there. Now she obeyed the summons with a different kind of dread: with anticipation and with disbelief that her present happy situation could endure.

She opened the door and stepped inside. There he sat behind the polished desk, dark and distinguished in his coat of claret velvet. Her heart lurched at the sight of him. In an instant Danville was on his feet, beckoning her forward. A chair in front of the desk was pulled out for her, and he bowed her wordlessly into it, seeing how the simple jonquil gown with its ruched collar set off her loveliness.

"You are prompt," he said, smiling and returning to his seat.

"How would I dare be otherwise, my lord?" she asked saucily, but her hands twisted together in her lap.

"You must learn to call me by my name rather than 'sirring' and 'my lording' me to death. My friends call me Fitz and my mother called me Evelyn."

"Yes, sir, but I would not presume to call you either one," she asserted soberly.

He lifted a brow. "We will say more on that head later. For now, I sent for you to read a letter I received from Nick Venner." He took the letter from the desk and came around it to give it to her. Laura received it in her lap; she was unable to hold the paper because her hand was shaking. She bent her head over it, the words blurring as she read. But the last sentences seemed to leap out at her.

My dear Fitz,

Today I had returned to me a trinket that I had rather not see again, although at one time I had every pawnshop in London on the lookout for it. I was desperate to find the person on whom I had forced it and whose distress I had caused. Later I came to hope that possession of the necklace might facilitate the lady's escape. The knowledge that she is safely home and under your enviable and unexceptionable protection relieves my mind.

I regret that period. Had I not been blinded by ennui and habitual cynicism, I might have come to admire Laura properly for her extraordinary worth as well as for the beauty of her person. At least I have come away a wiser man.

If I am released by this infernal bone-setter in time, I go to Caroline's wedding in London and then on to Venice. Perhaps after that you will have lost the impulse to plant me a facer.

Yrs,
Nick

Danville leaned against the desk as she read, his eyes on the shining mass of her hair. Laura looked up. "Caroline's wedding? I—I thought that you and Miss Venner—that is . . ." Her voice trailed off.

"Caroline and I? Indeed not. I became aware of her treacherous dealing with you. She exposed you deliberately to that hound Greystan. No, I am on the catch for another lady and hoping that she will join her life with mine."

Laura stared, her heart in her eyes. What was he saying?

"Can you not understand, dear goose? She has eyes like blue lakes and a stout heart as steady as time."

Laura's jaws clenched, and she bit hard on the inside of her cheek. She tasted salt in her mouth. Surely he was making a game of her, and how very cruel it was.

"It does not become you to tease me." She heard her own voice tremble.

"Tease you, my girl? Nothing could be more nonsensical. It becomes me to seek to marry you, a girl of natural goodness and uncommon turn of mind, if she will only have me."

Laura did not see how well the expression of hope and happiness on his countenance became him. He looked at her as if he could never get enough of the sight.

"I— You are funning. It is unthinkable. You forget that I am a servant. Do not—do not demean yourself and me." He is going beyond the bounds of reason, she thought.

"There is bound to be a clamor," he admitted. "It will pass. Let anyone speak out of turn, and I shall know how to give a proper set-down." Laura glanced up to see a softened look on his dark face, "The hub of the matter is that I love you. I must have you near me and I don't wish to live without you."

Feeling as if she were dreaming, Laura twisted her head from side to side. "Impossible!" She must not listen to the words he uttered, she thought hopelessly.

Danville spoke softly above her head. "I knew I would have my work cut out for me. I feel for you real love in all its depth and fullness, a need to give and to receive."

"How can you say that, you who have such pride of name and position?"

"Are you suggesting that I am stuffed up with my own consequence? I'll have you know, my girl, that even before you were taken away from me, I had formed the desire to place you by my side. My mother's love for you and my obligation to protect you forbade my thinking of you in any other light than that of wife. For a long time I fought that desire, thinking that my mother was mistaken in her high regard for you. It was slow, but I came unconsciously to value you as well as to wish to kiss that full proud mouth of yours." She heard him catch his breath. "When you were gone, I knew the full extent of my loss."

"I—I am afraid to believe you," whispered Laura.

"Think instead of the discomfort I might be facing."

"What do you mean?" She raised her head, showing traces of tears on her white cheeks.

"In having such a mantrap for a wife. But depend upon it, I shall be always on my guard." He laughed at her in gentle ridicule. She began to take in the fact that he was indeed serious.

"You have never spoken of the time I was with Nicholas," she whispered.

"Have done!" he ground out, his control breaking

as he dragged her up from the chair. He lifted her into his arms and strode to the alcove where she had sat writing for many hours after the death of Lady Danville. There he set her on her feet before the marble fireplace. "I have not spoken of it, nor shall I be able to for some time. When I allow myself to think of the liberties he took with you, I could run him through."

She looked up into a face suddenly savage, his eyes black with rage. She hid her face in the velvet of his coat. "I—I hated it!"

"Hate this, then!" His arms tightened cruelly as he pulled her toward him. She felt his hard frame against her legs as his mouth met hers in a down-driving kiss that ground her lips against her teeth. There was a thundering in her ears as she tried to breathe. Slowly the pressure eased as his tongue drove past her teeth. Laura was lost in a sensation that filled her with excitement and longing. She hung there in his embrace, and when he lifted his head to regard her intently, her whole face turned a scorching pink.

"Could you love me?" he demanded.

"I—I do," she breathed, too shy to raise her lids and see the glowing look on his face.

Drawing an uneven breath, he began to caress the back of her neck while his thumb stroked behind her ear. "I want your gentleness and your courage with me always as well as in our children. Nobody has complete happiness, but you and I shall have as near as there is to it."

Laura could not speak; she was lost in physical pleasure. Sparks ran through her body at the feel of his hand on her neck.

"Perhaps it would be better to have your portrait

done by Lawrence rather than Hoppner," he said
slowly, as if he had been thinking of it for some time.
"He deals better in oils, I think."

Laura blinked at him and tried to draw away.
"No! I shan't know how to go on in your world!" Was
it possible, she thought, that she had caught the
interest of this worldly and articulate man with all
his confidence and power? Scores of women had
blushed and bridled and tried to draw him to their
sides.

"Nonsense!" he said matter-of-factly. "Merely
learn to talk flowery commonplaces with the ladies
and to fend off the gentlemen. Mrs. Russell can help
you. But first you must learn to ride. Mrs. Meers is
ordering you a riding habit. I know that my mother
would have rejoiced with us."

He means it, she thought. He is deaf to argument.
She reached up shyly and put her fingertips on his
face, feeling the hard bone of his jaw clench under
her touch. He nipped her ring finger between his
teeth and bit down before he released it.

"With a ring for this finger I shall thee wed." The
words, spoken in his low resolute tones, sounded like
the marriage service.